This PICTURE DOESN'T HANG STRAIGHT

ADRIAN VOGT

Copyright © 2019 Adrian Vogt.

All rights reserved. No part of this book may be used or reproduced by any means, graphic, electronic, or mechanical, including photocopying, recording, taping or by any information storage retrieval system without the written permission of the author except in the case of brief quotations embodied in critical articles and reviews.

LifeRich Publishing is a registered trademark of The Reader's Digest Association, Inc.

LifeRich Publishing books may be ordered through booksellers or by contacting:

LifeRich Publishing
1663 Liberty Drive
Bloomington, IN 47403
www.liferichpublishing.com
1 (888) 238-8637

Because of the dynamic nature of the Internet, any web addresses or links contained in this book may have changed since publication and may no longer be valid. The views expressed in this work are solely those of the author and do not necessarily reflect the views of the publisher, and the publisher hereby disclaims any responsibility for them.

Any people depicted in stock imagery provided by Getty Images are models, and such images are being used for illustrative purposes only.
Certain stock imagery © Getty Images.

ISBN: 978-1-4897-2264-5 (sc)
ISBN: 978-1-4897-2263-8 (hc)
ISBN: 978-1-4897-2262-1 (e)

Library of Congress Control Number: 2019942732

Print information available on the last page. —————

LifeRich Publishing rev. date: 06/05/2019

Prologue

On this late Autumn evening the Moon hung low in the Sky, in the forefront of a shadowy Frontier. His hiding place was secure, where Fox and Rabbit would say "Goodnight" to one another.

Johannes knew that it was a matter of time before the enemy came for him and his team. The team – the Remnant Faithful - had long split up and went their separate ways and "off the grid."

He could hold off the Band of Killers for a short time. They drove armored vehicles, carried the latest weaponry, and were battle seasoned.

He knew why they wanted to kill him, his wife and his team.

The conspiracy of the Corporate Front First to control the three largest economic segments – Banking and Finance, Big Pharma and Food Services, was discovered by the examination team during a routine examination of the New York branch of one of the largest private Banks in Germany.

Alistair O'Bannon and his Brazilian wife, Rosa hired a band of Iraq War veterans to silence the team and all of its known accomplices.

Their Plans would soon go awry because of one individual - Miguelito Pohlmann, a Cuban Refugee and survivor of the brutal communist regime of Fidel Castro.

He made certain that he could erase all potential threats against his loyal friends.

He was a soldier of the Lord. Miguelito Pohlmann knew that he could rely fully on God's legacy to him and all of mankind for success against the EVIL conjured up by the members of the Corporate Front First.

Plundered

He was of the opinion that Integrity is the lifeblood of democracy; in its veins is deception, a poison.

He thought about that arrogant politician, who spent almost 40 years in the U.S. Senate.

Eight years ago, he pontificated to the Media about the key reason for his success in the early years: "One of the things that I observed in the early days in Washington DC, is that one could take an argument of another person, and twist it to your advantage – even if untrue – and run with it!"

He also reiterated: "Of course, others eventually find out that it is not exactly accurate, then I change the argument to something else; this Method is very effective, I have used it many times."

Several reporters recall this conversation with this Bostonian, who openly admitted to establishing his own Dynasty.

This towheaded individual seldom enjoyed strenuous activity. He belonged to one of the most prosperous families in America. He would certainly have little idea about the sound of a 'hard-working" forklift truck.

Since he personally visited few production facilities in his own State, unless, election time was in the offing, then shake a few hands with labor union leaders could never hurt his image as a champion of the working people.

His growing popularity among the leadership was understandable; the lower paying service membership now far exceeded the number of remaining industrial members, and represented few, if any, individuals who were non-citizens.

And the subject of transparency continued not to be a problem for him and his family.

After his death in 2010, his Family made certain that all FBI investigative documents against this "Champion of the People" and other family members were permanently unavailable to the public.

Johannes Emmerich, a Federal Reserve Bank of New York Examiner, was very familiar with the Modus Operandi (MO) of this individual. He noted his penchant to create a sense of "deep confusion" to lead someone astray.

An undergraduate of Southern Methodist University, Dallas, Texas, Johannes attended several meetings of the "Young Republican" students in the Spring of 1960.

One meeting in particular, focused attention on a young, good looking Bostonian, campaigning for his brother to become the first catholic President of the USA.

This towheaded person stated clearly at this meeting that his brother would not cause a stop in the offshore drilling on the Texas coast. He added: efforts to reduce certain tax benefits for the industry would not occur. Of course, he lied.

As the new president's brother became senator, he recommended a cutback in those allowances so that the charge for depletion of oil and gas properties became less generous.

The deceptive political strategy was not new, as Adolph Hitler said: "tell a Lie loud enough and long enough, then the people will begin to believe it."

Nowadays it is normal, that one hears the whirr of many forklift trucks lurching forwards and backwards on the concrete floors of former production facilities as these magnificent machines easily lifted and stacked the large cartons of cheese, peanut butter, milk powder, rice, vegetables, noodles, cereals, processed meats, and soy protein.

These massive facilities provide storage of enormous quantities of foodstuffs for the growing customer base: the army of unemployed and the elderly poor.

In many of the former industrialized states, one can discover this new "growth industry." Business objective: quell Hunger.

Of course, new jobs are created for those wanting the opportunity to work. But the jobs created by this growth industry are without monetary compensation. Nevertheless, the new worker engages in this type of "feel good" occupation voluntarily – it is good for the soul.

This "feel good" work has expanded in the suburbs of the major cities in this land of endless American dreams of success.

Johannes noticed that the Senator also recognized a certain potential for him and his cronies. The stuff of political demonstrations and agitation for a fairer distribution of the national income!

Wait a minute! How can this be? The Senator represents a constituency of former employees of major corporations that moved their production overseas to ostensibly produce a less costly product for this "laid off" customer base!

Johannes could not be fooled by this talk; he remembered the words of his Priest: "Satan's work is to misrepresent people and situations and then to use his lies to encourage wrongful deeds. Many do not comprehend the multi-faceted levels of evil operating in your midst today."

Through his position of influence, the Senator sought self-gain and power through this new-found opportunity.

After all, he mused: "I can impose my own argument for reaching in to other people's pockets under the guise of feeding the children and those impacted by the great recession!"

"Angela, please get me the latest info on the Nation's Food Banks."

Angela, a staunch supporter of the Senator, came via a hidden tunnel across the California-Mexico Border. It wasn't an easy trip.

The Senator met her on the other side. She was a dark haired beauty, and most grateful to the towheaded gentleman.

One could imagine some intimate favors for him from her for this rather exciting trip through the tunnel.

One could also say that she repaid his kindness through hard work for his political machine.

His demeanor changed as she strolled through the doorway to his office and leaned over his mahogany wood desk, her thin white blouse revealed large chocolate colored nipples. She was again in the mood to reward his kindness.

"Senator, you will be surprised at the numbers," she purred.

Since her employment with the Senator, she made sure that her choice of perfumes would meet his approval.

The Report indicated that one of the largest food banks had over 200 locations, operated in all 50 states, the District of Columbia and Puerto Rico. Annual distribution of foodstuffs total 2.5 Billion pounds. About 38 million people are fed each year.

He thought of the large corporations and their displacement of so many jobs overseas. Ah, yes. They will be my donors for upcoming elections.

Oh yes, free markets, little regulation, these strategies benefit everyone, sighed the Senator.

A local newspaper displayed an artful caricature of the situation which did not please the Senator.

Cartoon-like, the picture showed several scratch wounds on the almost worn out body of a middle aged person, much like the artwork appearing in publications such as "Mad" and "Hustler."

Other critics of globalization parodied the requests for donations for the George W. Bush and/or Ronald Reagan presidential Libraries! These ex-presidents still received their pensions, courtesy of the U.S. taxpayer.

Who is the biggest Fool? These members of the world's second oldest profession think the voting public is.

Johannes observed the person polishing the hardwood floors of the executive suite at one of the institutions he was in the process of examining.

A friendly type, this service worker, originated from the area of Germany that Johannes used to live. In the days to come, Franz Schmid would be one of his strongest information gatherers.

This money market bank financed many transfers of production facilities to lesser developed countries, oversaw the dismissal of displaced employees, effectively became the outsourced personnel department of the stripped-down corporation.

Franz overheard conversations late at night in the executive suites of future opportunities for the long time worker – they would make recommendations for them to become waiters and waitresses at some of Manhattan's finest restaurants!

"What are they complaining about? Of course, the pay is less, but they have the privilege to still work with us!"

Franz was aghast at this remark.

He did not know his conspicuous ways, the Senator assisted only those persons where there might be some payback; in the case of immigrant women, there was always something; after all, the Senator only wanted his fair share of the "Good Life."

The Senator's offices were filled with the latest array of technology, which provided the latest trading information to him and his family.

Self- gain, power, popularity, are the end-objectives of the good-looking towhead.

He knew that he abused his authority to achieve his own brand of greatness. His actions would touch the lives of many, be it positive or negative.

"Well, "he reasoned, "I can do these things, because, well, I can!"

He thought about Angela's neckline, as he leaned over his own desk to click into the broad array of investment brokers to conclude a portion of the daily trades.

He observed in the extensive data bank of investment values which included the Great Depression; now, values were quite reasonable, he mused: "lower by some US 40 to 50 trillion worldwide."

A year after the "Bloodbath" the Senator promised the usual purveyors of Private Capital that he would recommend no additional taxes on their dividends: "Business as usual, my Brothers and Sisters!"

His favorite co-workers, mostly attractive women of various backgrounds, were encouraged to begin the work day one hour after sunrise. Most were "unattached."

"Remember, my beautiful colleagues, the first order of business is always our superb voting public," grinned the Senator.

On this day in April 2010, Johannes reflected on the dramatic swings in Asset values, which made the trading community and the politicians happy and VERY RICH.

More times than not, he thought, more is made after the waning days of a recession, than when the chicken has long flown the coop.

Outside he could see no more snow. He saw the Red Robin, the true Harbinger of Spring. He shouldn't feel depressed, he and Alischraga still lived, although in hiding.

He believed his feelings of dejection stemmed from his past. He still heard the metallic thud of that crash that changed his life forever; mild PTSD and those periodic visions haunted him.

Alischraga gave him courage; she had saved his Life. It also occurred to him that the common freedoms enjoyed by most, could quickly disappear!

The Senator and his Donors wanted to hold some Freedoms in check: the middle class was disappearing, their jobs were being offered overseas.

They were abusing the Divine Will of our Creator through their short-sighted Self-Gain. They lulled the public with their Exhortations of Innovation and empty Promises: "If re-elected, the best days of our Nation are before us!"

In Johannes' thoughts reverberated: Wisdom of Solomon. "For the Lord of all will not stand in awe of anyone, nor show deference to greatness; because He himself made both small and great, and He takes thought for all alike. But a strict inquiry is in store for the mighty."

He yelled out: "they are sticking us in a Global Prison! The remaining Remnant of the middle class will be viewed as rich and prosperous by the voting public who may acquiesce to the politician's demands for higher taxes to assuage the growing army of low wage earners!"

Reality?

The planned displacement of high wage jobs and their elimination domestically in favor of lower paying jobs in services?

Who will maintain the pace of Re-distribution of the National Income?

Is this the "New Slavery?" The "New Tyranny?"

Johannes' colleagues enjoyed these controversial topics – especially after work over drinks.

They shared his Concerns.

They belonged to the survivors of Financial Terrorism; they are the New Generation of Financial Institution Examiners, which are in the position, once and for all, to eliminate the "New Feudalism."

"The government elites want to control the consumption habits of all citizens; the Central Bank, the Food and Drug Administration and other agencies, whose strategy is to promote propaganda through Confusion and Fear. "

"They are fighting to influence your consumption decisions that affect your Body and Soul."

Their Mantra is for scientific findings to direct the purchasing power to "Big Pharma" and its campaign to always have something in the Pipeline of new drugs.

As a corollary to Big Pharma is the continued success of the processed foods industry, whose inclination is to favor shelf life and profit over the true nutritional value of foods.

The team agreed that the Senator's deceptive strategy was directed by satanic forces that foster the destruction of individual sovereignty.

Sound teaching of the Truth is no longer popular – only the worship of philosophies that suit the liking of the Elite.

The team knew the pitfalls of following truthful principles of Regulation. The actual resolution of problems within the regulated industries was resisted by their own managements.

Several years ago, Johannes found his Focus on his work was being challenged; the growing Corruption in the Finance-and Agriculture segments troubled him.

On the one hand, fewer families could afford fresh food; the incidence of malnutrition and disease conditions began to increase, and, prices of pharmaceuticals and so-called health care became price inelastic.

The heat in Johannes large body started to rise, as he continued to review the consequences of unbridled corruption: the dilution of work incentives and middle class work led to economic inequality and faulty consumption priorities.

In the meantime, the donors – the usual suspects – as we now affectionately call them, rewarded themselves with hefty Bonuses for their acumen and effort to bring the country back from the Brink of Disaster!

The Senator and his donors responded to this environment by recommending better education to equip oneself for the jobs of tomorrow!

It was all too obvious for the Team that something wasn't right: the large picture didn't hang right! Who and what would re-align the picture?

The Business journals all reported the reduction in domestic factory jobs, and applications for work continued their downward spiral.

The clever analysts began to revise their language for explaining the earnings future of a company traded on exchanges.

They would opine that revenues are better than expected! Although the trend might continue negative!

Johannes said: "The Concept of a huge Charade and financial terrorism still lives, it thrives on the Lethargy and the Ignorance of the taxpayer!"

It was December 2009. It was breezy and a cold rain ensued. Outside Johannes rubbed his hands vigorously to offset the drop in internal temperature.

The storefronts displayed Christmas decorations made in the USA!

Inside he leafed through various catalogues, and noticed that most toys and Christmas ornaments were made not in the USA, but in those countries where the least cost methods dominated. And the price per item was marked the same as those displayed "made in the USA!"

The producer wanted its share; actually, more than its fair share, since the profit margin expanded. No rebate to the consumer.

Johannes heard the familiar sound of Christmas music, the ringing bells, the Choir of voices under the grey winter sky, sweet as those birds that hibernate the Winter.

This group of Christian Soldiers wore the same dark blue uniforms, and for their generous, caring work, received no Bonus payments for their charitable work.

Johannes' thoughts returned to present day issues; the team has left. They remain convinced that operational changes have to be made.

The first day of January started early like all others.

He enjoyed Bio-Coffee with his beautiful wife, Alischraga, reviewed the usual business magazines which all indicated that the financial crisis only became worse due to the lackluster performances of the Elite.

Johannes and his team had long memories of those who were traitors to the "Cause."

On their "Shit List" were those comments: "the Experts and their Economic Protectors were liars!"

"They fucked us royally!"

They remembered:

"March and August 2007, declared the Pols and their Regulators that the real estate markets remained robust; the economy characterized as "stable."

One large Investment Fund even had the nerve to advertise "Gain from our Perspective!"

Suddenly Johannes thought of Alistair and Fernanda. They still held on to their positions. They had already cashed their Bonuses.

The Plunderers. They only wanted their Share!

They and their Insiders engaged almost endlessly in Short Sales.

They understood the mechanics of the Collateralized Debt Obligation, had privy to the collateral and the activity within the collateral supporting the repayment.

The Rating Agencies provided them more information that they needed to ascertain 'realistic" default ratios.

Long considered "Shit stats" by those in the know, they could harvest enormous gains via the short sale.

Johannes knew also that to make matters worse, those all-knowing Fucks with the prestigious European Banks only relied on the Rating Agency Bullshit ; performing little credit analysis of their own!

Their typical response to their Press people: "there is no occasion for great concern!"

"The U.S. Real Estate Crisis will not become an uncontrollable Grass Fire!"

"Freddie Mac and Fannie Mae are fundamentally sound, they are in good shape going forward."

Two months later, in September 2008, both were bailed out with $100 billion...each.

Johannes and the team rummaged through stacks of periodicals: Business Week,Time, Wall Street Journal, Frankfurter Allgemeine Zeitung, Profil, Handelsblatt, Financial Times, etc. and almost word for word, the same comments:

"There is no basis for a cascading effect, but individual companies may be impacted, those who behaved too aggressively, the markets would quiet down relatively quickly."

"No danger to us via the U.S Mortgage Crisis."

"The German Financial Branch can withstand the Crisis. Our "real economy" is very robust."

"A stock market crash is likewise not to be feared."

The comments continue unabated. The Team became very suspicious that they must act quickly to alert Alistair and Fernanda, their Superiors.

They looked to Johannes for a reply. He said, "Read further, and consider the sources."

A litany of near-unity comments encouraged more speculation that all was not well, and justified the team's suspicions.

"The capital market conditions will gradually normalize again, we call on all participants to remain calm."

"The crisis will endure until the Fall of the Year, but will scarcely influence the German economy."

"In no case, should we call forth any potential problem with the German banks, and with that unsettle the markets."

Bill, one of the most capable Examiners on the Team, replied: "Look here, Johannes, perhaps we might be able to re-think the Situation with the politicians, the banks, and resolve regulatory questions."

His sarcasm was not lost; in a word: everything needed Revision. A Helluva lot of it.

The team could certainly agree on one issue: beyond the typical economic statistics, one hears about, most of the time government officials simply don't know what they are talking about.

Bill, a hulk of a man, was an excellent dresser. He wore dark suits and mostly stripped shirts. Paisley ties were the rule, not the exception.

Everything that revolved around the stability of financial markets occupied center stage.

Johannes noticed that the new Chairman of the Board of Governors seemed uncomfortable during his first meeting before the Senate Finance Committee. His hairy hands gestured wildly as he described the financial crisis.

He described eloquently the tragic events affecting various families, and he made no secret of the fact that the giant mountain of global debt was absolutely necessary.

Johannes mumbled: O.K.

He listened to the questions from the Committee. The answers given were those of a person very astute in the liquidity aspects relating to a financial crisis.

On the table he arranged several Federal Reserve Notes.

On each Note appeared the signatures of prior Treasurers, all members of that Group, which played a major role to control the political Destiny of the Nation. Unfortunately, since its Founding this Cadre of individuals focused more on self- aggrandizement over the years than the National Well-Being.

They wore the veil of misuse of National Resources and their power amounted to a Compromise of the Truth: An avid partner of the planned moral decay, which today is happening worldwide.

Johannes Emmerich was convinced that few individuals live for the common salvation of our global Soul.

The huge mess created in the financial markets could have been avoided. In Unison they inquired: "How?"

He replied: "Simple. Pay off all mortgage holders with the Federal Bailout package. The Collateral held consisted of Prime and Sub-prime loans."

"However, our Management did not heed our warnings since

the year 1995 – the birth year of the new Risk Asset Examination principles, that every CDO must be examined as to ultimate Collectability and recovery of asset values, if the overall Economy tanked!"

"The quasi-Nationalization of major banks and major industry segments was the ultimate choice of the politician, the Congress made it easy for all those who wanted their immediate fair share!"

"Courtesy of the global taxpayer!"

The long standing Charade unfolded not easily, it could be compared to a large amount of washed clothing on an outside clothes line to dry.

Unfortunately, many of the still hanging clothes have become dry and stiff. The water drops have long fallen to the ground, and like dog shit already transformed into toxic dust blowing everywhere.

Bill's Comparison of the increasingly "loose" Regulatory environment that permitted the on-going Evaporation of Value drew raucous laughter from the team.

"Ripped off" by their Government and the financial Lobbyists would be an understatement, thought Johannes.

A few years before the crisis, the Dominoes began to cascade. Other entities and their stakeholders would feel pain.

They knew the Charade was alive and well as they read the Eulogy for the one-time Chairman of Enron Corporation.

The ex-President of the USA joined others to refer to the deceased as a great role model for life, business and the Christian Faith!

Not mentioned were the suffering shareholders, pensioners, investors, banks, and others who lost most of their funds in the now defunct entity, chaired by that great Benefactor of the Houston, Texas community.

Some sold, others held on with the hope of recovery: From $90 a share in mid- 2000 to a $1.00 a share in November 2001.

Basic accounting and management principles were not observed by the Board of Directors, nor were the right questions asked and answers to these vigorously pursued.

Johannes: "clearly, the Bulldog Rule was not in place."

One of the team was dubbed the Bulldog because of his pleasant persistent way of obtaining information.

Bill: "Where were the regulators?"

"Wow! Was 2001 not one hell of a year for bad shit?"

"Even the mathematical modelling was never in the position of being able to measure and forecast the enormous amount of delinquent mortgage payments!"

Bill added: "The days of broad customer diversification of credit cards and mortgage debt of poor credit risk are long gone. Also, a substantial number of new borrowers do not have a credit history since coming from other countries with little credit reporting and monitoring systems."

"Of course, the quality of underlying documents and properties to satisfactorily support the mortgage debt remains questionable."

He added: "The substitution of collateral also became a 'flash point', in that the bank's man-power was intentionally ratcheted down to lower variable expense, AND who among the regulators would ever invest the time to "check out" the collateral?!"

Bill took the line that the banks really did not know the tenacity of the team. "Wait 'till they get a load of us!!"

Johannes took a deep breath, and said:

"The Politicians really screwed the pooch! The regulators continued their new policy of American style Democracy: behind closed doors decisions for the good of the Country, or should we say, to further rely on the tax payer."

Johnny D (JD), known as the Bulldog to his colleagues, his cat like hazel-green eyes beaming, entered the room.

About six foot tall, slicked back dark hair, and always well dressed, he grinned and stated: "Hey, guys and gals, we got to ask the right questions, to address this so-called Financial Armageddon."

"How much is this Shit now worth?"

He didn't mince words. He always relied on drawing simple diagrams and T-accounts to demonstrate the issue. Simple.

Many investors witnessed the daily plundering as reported by the Media and the Gossipmongers.

The junior Senator from Massachusetts screamed: "we have to deal with this Crap in a reasonable way!"

Johannes watched her speak as the foam began to form around her rounded pursed lips. "Wow, is she really cranked up!"

But her solution made good sense: Pay off all debtors and the total debt becomes whole. Finally, a politician that uttered good sense, he thought.

But the usual suspects wouldn't hear of it.

They belonged to the many who hold hidden agendas in their hearts, clearly their guile would prevent them from climbing the pinnacle of truth – truth is the victory over all lies and error.

Bill went to the window and looked out at the cloudy and overcast sky, it looked like snow. J.D. followed.

Bill looked concerned and said: "that sky contains so much toxic dust from the transportation, people farting in their all too unconventional clothing, the Mist now falling from the pollutants of those noisy Iron Birds…"

He stopped talking.

He thought of the actor, Farah Fawcett, who had lost her long battle with the 'Big C" in 2009. Two years before, the renowned German actor, Ulrich Muehe, also succumbed to that dreaded Sickness.

Both of these individuals, like most, tried to lead a healthy life; but in reality, this goal is difficult to achieve, since the toxic clouds emitted by some industries globally circulate.

The Board rooms are filled with men and women interested only in the "bottom line", rather than the global health of nations. They dare not fall off the treadmill of their superficial existence.

This debt to humanity, like all other debt, must eventually be repaid!

How is THIS debt to be repaid?

Bill now knew why "Big Pharma" demonstrated year after year profit gains; funded by the pollution of the environment, the propaganda of their lobbyists, that everyone is entitled to health care and medical attention: the cash cow became fatter and fatter!

Even more so, as the world's population continued to grow, most populous regions could not control their environment, they never heard of pollution control devices for factories and autos, in any case, the multi-national companies would keep them informed of their own progress to climb out of the "third world hole."

Ah, yes. Education and information are powerful tools to control people, mused the corporate dictators, all members of the CFF.

Back home in their board rooms, the usual suspects recognized the guaranteed inflation of their Drug Industry, they only paid 'lip service" to the sinking wages of the middle class, and they championed the idea of less expensive goods from overseas: "save more, spend less and live better."

That phrase served to only "piss off" the knowledgeable taxpayer, whose income bracket was being re-classified upward by the politicians and the tax authorities.

The tyranny of this industry as demonstrated by the relentless pursuit of new drugs whose side effects might well offset any measurable benefit became acceptable!

Bill and JD walked back in to the Board Room, which was provided by bank management for their examination of the institution's financial strength, and viewed the stacks of bulky files and folders of the bank's corporate customers.

Among the stack one could see that many were the major players of Big Pharma.

Bill and JD reviewed several of the memoranda prepared by the account officers. Court cases proved to be the most informative.

One case was especially enlightening.

One teenaged boy was restricted by the State of Minnesota court to only chemotherapy for his advanced cancer. Alternative treatments were not allowed, as those considered by the family were deemed by the medical elite as "unproven" and "quackery."

The court ordered the family to not seek other treatment.

However, the memo pointed out the favorable results of other treatments – Laetrile, other non-toxic cancer treatments instead of toxic chemotherapy and radiation.

The family escaped to Mexico for the alternative treatment performed by highly trained medical professionals. The result for their son was favorable.

JD turned to the others, and said: "Wow! Do we live in a democracy or a medical dictatorship?"

Johannes reviewed a file entitled "Dr. Matthias Rath, Physician and Alternative Medicine practitioner."

The credit history was very favorable, repayments always punctual and even a "clean up" period for the credit line was voluntarily observed by Dr. Rath!

"Unheard of, most borrowers would almost never pay down annually, preferring instead to put their debt on an "evergreen" status, said Johannes.

He continued to read through the file, noting that in 2006, the Doctor was subjected to a judicial inquiry accusing him of being a "Charlatan" in the medical field, his shrinkage of tumors using "natural substances" were not proven and amounted to 'quackery", claimed his medical and drug company accusers. They wanted him to cease his practice because it gave false hope to cancer patients and was a danger to the public!

To counter the negative talk of the medical monopoly, the judge requested the opinion of Dr. Med. Georg Mayr, University of Hamburg, since he conducted extensive research on the benefits of polyphenols, a large family of natural compounds widely distributed in plant foods.

After discussing his opinion, that these substances are necessary for Cancer prevention, and most have anti-carcinogenicity properties, the Judge threw out the case against Dr. Rath, and stated that his research gave an honest and very worthy contribution to the alternative ways of fighting Cancer."

He added: "the Media's information on the case against Dr. Rath was completely unfounded and based on many untruths."

The team unanimously rated Dr. Rath's credit risk to the bank as low – a satisfactory/strong ability to fully repay his debt at any time.

MPAG's New York branch's total assets were quite large, and the number of files to review would probably enable the team to finish their work in about 6 weeks.

Alistair O'Bannon, Senior Vice President with the New York District, was not pleased that the team was reviewing a very large sample of credit files at the New York branch of this large private bank headquartered in Frankfurt, Germany.

Alistair was overruled in his objections by the Committee chaired by one of his arch-rivals, another immigrant from Northern Ireland, who became the favorite to become the next Head of the Bank Supervision and Regulation division.

Alistair did not like the team to review the files relating to Big Pharma; this would cramp his style – that is, hinder his extensive insider trading, and might mean the delay to certain plans for an IPO providing funds for the promising field of irradiation technology.

Basis: he knew alternative treatments were the next revolution, and profit margins would surely decline as any new so-called medical advance in the treatment of disease would not be patentable.

Natural healing substances needed no patents, they were plentiful through Nature's gifts, he reasoned.

This development really pissed him off!

There is a way out, thought Alistair.

The dissemination of "fake news" or propaganda thrown out to the public about new and recurring diseases and the potential harmful bacteria burdening the nation's food supply would become his new mantra.

After all, who would challenge it? At least enable sufficient time for launching his IPO.

Alistair thought about his early immigrant days; America, I love America and her lobbyists and eager government chums.

He grinned further as he read the article in Fortune magazine about his former boss, and how he relieved his sore back symptoms sitting in the bath tub reading business journals, etc.

23

Bullshit!

The author of this article didn't know the real reason: that horny bastard was busy consistently boning that younger wife!

His thoughts carried him to the so-called free market which enabled some to achieve quick returns of 25% or more annually in their core banking activities, we are wearing the masks of famous bandits as the Congress has given us license to conduct business in such a way that it wouldn't be considered "illegal."

The 2008/2009 crisis was driven by the same bandits, financial terrorists, the same people overseeing a substantial dose of operational negligence, would soon harvest an enormous profit from the taxpayer funds set aside to stave off another Great Depression!

Unbridled Corporate power! Like the giant Gorilla, who could jump from one tree to the next, because he could!!

But this situation plagued Johannes and his Team.

Who will have the courage to compel the unlawful to deviate from their immoral behavior? Would it be possible to switch their behavior to something else, to change the rules of their Game? So that the Heirs do not carry forward this distorted philosophy?

At present, the usual suspects – the financial giants and investment firms, that pass off most risk to the investor, keeping little risk for their own books, are really driving the Bus.

Also belonging to this Cabal, are the Keynesians at prestigious universities, former U.S. Presidents, Treasury Secretaries, ex-New York Federal Reserve Bank Presidents, Chairmen of Economic Advisers, and Budget Directors.

End result: the government regulates Nothing, it is governed by the usual suspects, whose game is to create Conflict and Volatility for higher shareholder value. Globally.

Succinctly put: they piss with the Big Dogs!

This was one of those days that Johannes felt uncertain and behaved erratically.

And, for good reason.

He looked out the window of his hiding place at the very large Doberman, which rested at the foot of an enormous oak tree whose branches appeared to reach into the Heavens.

It thrived during the days of the American Revolution.

Johannes noticed a difference in the color tone of the tree. The base of the tree was dull and he could see thin brown, red and yellow stripes which tended to rise upward. The inside of this huge tree was long scraped clean by termites, and this enormous wooden shell somehow still stood. The parasites coveted the sticky sweet sap and they consumed slowly and steadily until fully sated. They finally got their fair share.

The ground under this deeply rooted tree appeared ash grey in color, which meant that it was not fertile, moisture absorption was out of the question, no amount of fertilizer, pesticides, GMO seeds, even large doses of radiation could save the soil; anything to save this once mighty landmark would be welcome.

Could it ever be healthy again under the ever-changing "New Environment" and her radically altered conditions?

The Doberman raised his large head, and looked up at Johannes.

He remembered the Doberman. It glowered long at him, eyes like red-hot coals. Johannes became motionless from fear. Perspiration covered his face, he knew why he was now very uncomfortable.

Satan's job is to cause confusion, provoke trouble and unrest! This is his hallmark.

Johannes thought of the team, they had dispersed quickly, after Alistair and Fernanda showed their true colors. He did not know where they had gone. Their respective hiding places he also did not know. One day, they would come together stronger than ever.

The "remnant faithful" as we now can refer to the team, is ready to counter Satan's mentality of deep confusion and lack of understanding of the rules of time-proven godly principles: the great gift of choosing a form of government that focuses on biblical principles.

They would re-group and perform once again their outstanding analysis of financial entities and bolster the overall integrity of the American financial system - on their terms, the application of righteous authority.

He looked where the Doberman had been. He peered through the broad window, and saw something else: A voluptuous brunette. She wore a stripped mini-skirt, as she strolled slowly, a soft breeze lifted it just so, to give the viewer a sensuous picture of real beauty, or, at least so the person thought.

She wore heels, very high heels, which accentuated her "larger than life" appearance. But she still had not mastered the walk with these especially fashionable shoes. With each step she tended to rock from side to side.

The American flag appeared on the mini-skirt; even the stars sparkled, – she demonstrated a quite unusual physical figure, noted Johannes.

Other pedestrians on this heavily trafficed street noticed her; perhaps they found her "sporty-looking." In any case, she is "stacked."

Enough now, he thought.

He remembered that day he saw a dark spot on Fernanda's office carpet. Was it blood or mud?

He looked at it closer, underneath the spot appeared an amount of tiny fissures, which were not connected!

Something wasn't right, he thought.

But the dark spot disturbed him; he found himself mesmerized. What was the reason for his sudden attention to this inanimate thing?

Suddenly he recalled the sensuous nature of the Creature. He looked carefully at the dirt under the fissures.

He wanted a quick explanation. He demanded ONE!

His better Self pointed to something else: his Psyche was poisoned! His Mind was broken – fucked up!

His breathing began to race; or was it something more sinister? Like immediate satisfaction – an expression of self- love!

Like wanting something NOW! The passion of constant shopping, purchasing STUFF! This thought haunted him.

The Creature now wore a large sign- held in place by her large breasts, it smelled of cheap perfume, sweet smelling – the Ad was convincing, if not alluring.

The Creature knew the number of onlookers began to multiply, as she suddenly threw her jogging bra to the crowd, it starred at the surprised expressions on the faces of her audience, she held them in her spell, when she raised her skirt to display her "Commando" status!

It reveled in the attention, it used its tongue to moisten its thick red lips, it craved the attention of everyone to agitate their individual fantasy.

It became agitated and angry at Johannes, he would regret ignoring me, it thought. "Johannes did not understand that I am really a very sensitive creature", it mused.

"Up to now, my strategy is working: first, I draw the public's attention to me through my glitzy clothing, secondly, my smooth skin will be shown. The crowd of "Gawkers," are just that – stupid. They will be held in my rapture!"

It laughed lustily as more sensual words flowed from her large, round mouth:

"I have been here more than twenty years."

"I felt like I was in prison, it was evil to hold me in such a narrow place."

"Now, I am unchained, I can revel in PLEASURE, untamed, like an angry Bitch Dog."

"Running around – now unrestrained."

Johannes continued to watch the Spectacle.

It had enticed several hundred onlookers.

Then it disappeared. Poof! Like a Fart in the Wind.

It had haunted him for years. How did it enter his Psyche?

Or was it because of certain medications for his PTSD that caused him to hallucinate and simulate panic attacks?

Unbeknownst to Johannes, Alistair also viewed the Creature and its sensual machinations from his spacious office. The miniskirt seemed a smidgen too small for her upper body; genuine Titts, pushed upward, what more would any real man want?

Anyone not finding it attractive would most likely bat for the other team, he thought. Such a voluptuous being, or so he thought.

In reality, Alistair was a financial terrorist, and devoted a fair amount of time to obtaining his fair share of the "Fairer sex."

Difference: he was not a terrorist of fine female skin, he admired greatly the good Lord's creation.

It would take some time for the truth to surface. In the meantime he would arbitrage the time difference of Fact and Fiction into real money – like that fucking Senator.

The middle class is learning a bitter lesson about low-cost production and how their jobs were sacrificed on the Altar of corporate shareholder value and political correctness.

They sensed something was not right with this picture – it didn't hang straight.

Their questions about this disturbing mess became more frequent. Alistair was sympathetic to their needs. An immigrant

ADRIAN VOGT

from Ireland, he never forgot the oppressive British rule, the IRA uprisings, and the new Peace that might endure.

They wanted answers!

Why not produce here? Why must we buy patented seeds from giant corporations?

Why do our elected officials not stop these bastards from taking our livelihood away from us?

Those Pricks with their tax-payer funded perks throw only salt in the wounds of the laid off worker as they would prefer to discuss the symptoms rather than the underlying Cause of this lost "Lifestyle".

The politicians do not lose time to show their faces on the ever more revered "Tube" and its myriad of 'true life" situations fed ever more by the FKA's of midnight pontifications: the pols speak only superfluous junk whose main purpose is to always show their leering faces on talk shows.

Talk, talk, talk to a stupid element of the public that continues to fund the lifestyles of the rich and famous pols.

Smoke and mirrors.

Basic economics shows us that a higher per capita income provides a higher living standard, real demand, political stability, and for the national Treasury, reliable sources of tax revenue!

Alistair had already reaped substantial benefit from the Politics of Deceit and Half-truths that governs the nation. Alistair knew the game.

Satanic obstruction and opposition carried out by the Corporate

First Front (CFF) which mission is to provide an environment for their own existence, without which the ultimate objective of their own brand of global domination would not be possible.

In their own unwritten "Rules of the Road", the biblical foundations of the founding Fathers must be labeled as "irrelevant" and not founded on worldly or secular principles.

However, the CFF knew that America's first civil government was based on a covenant with God.

The Mayflower Compact: "We come to this nation to propagate the Gospel of Jesus Christ and to establish good government, based on HIS principles, and we covenant with God to do that."

No other government has been founded in this way. Americans were the first people in 2000 years to choose whether the righteous would rule or the evil doers.

Johannes and his team fought for these ideals, the middle class, effective – not oppressive-regulation, and, unfortunately try to convince their management that social reality in the long run would reject the unchecked tyranny of the Elitist Modus Operandi.

Johannes compared the elitist CFF to a dinner host that only talked about his or her accomplishments the entire evening, "stole" morsels from their and other's plates, kicked you under the table, showed no concern for your well-being, and then gives you, the guest, the check for the evening.

That early Fall evening the weather conditions became unpleasant: storm clouds moved in quickly, and Media reports indicated a global phenomenon occurring.

Soon the rapidly increasing Strikes of Lightening would find their prey, the octopus like tentacles splintered the underlying trees, violent waves of wind driven rain flooded the valleys, and these soon came under water, lots of water, and the valleys once again became pristine.

The flood of anger and unrest is coming, but when? When has a person had enough – wondered Johannes.

Alistair wiped the tiny pearls of sweat from the naked brown body of his wife, Rosa.

The action had come and gone.

From the patio door he saw the sun come up, the Gulf of Mexico which surrounded the Cayman Islands, reflected rays of gold transcending one color after another, depending on the time of day.

As private citizens, Alistair and his very wealthy wife, held in high esteem the U.S. Treasury Guidelines for offshore accounts, at least for a part of their entire wealth.

As he sauntered away from the balcony, inhaling the salt air, with closed eyes, thinking of not much, he heard his "smart phone" ring. The message did not provide him a good perspective of the future.

Johannes and his wife had eluded capture and certain death, thanks to that Cuban fellow who had bumped off the small army of Iraq veterans hired by Alistair and Rosa.

On the other end of the phone, a very nervous voice said:

"Yeah, reeely awd dat people tawld meee dat dey herd weeerd noiisses lak eh primawl screeem aefterr day gon shawts – lak eh reeely pissed awf sumwan!

He continud his "antsy drawl" saying he first observed all bodies, then when he returned with the police and body bags, they were no longer on the ground!

"Lak eh faaart eenda Weeend – Whooosh!"

That statement unnerved Rosa. Who were they now dealing with?

Under cover, Alischraga and her husband were in the kitchen making Espresso. Johannes took the "Café Bustelo" container from the refrigerator, opened the can, poured the aromatic contents into a glass jar to maintain its freshness.

Johannes starred at the date on the bottom of the aluminum container. September 11, 2011, ten years had passed.

In the deepest part of his brain, lay the helpless screams of many victims, the highest floors of the North Tower were impacted to the point that escape was not an option.

They could only watch the burning aluminum shards and office paper shreds before they had to make life or death survival decisions: jump, be burned alive, or seek in vain, alternate escape routes which did not exist.

Others could only hope to jump to lower floors grabbing anything to cushion their descent. Escape from the toxic dust was not possible. Others in their desperate journey from the hot flames would end up as splattered tomatoes on the ground below.

One day the living victims would still suffer from not knowing why this had happened. A conspiracy theory could not be fully discarded.

Alischraga took from her Johannes the cup of Espresso, and noticed that his forehead was covered in shiny beads of sweat.

She had lived daily with his pain, remembered that night, when he finally arrived home. He resembled a snowman: everything he wore was white with asbestos and toxic concrete dust. Everything had to be incinerated.

They observed the constant re-runs of the events of 9/11/2001and wondered aloud about other areas of stress: the rights of people and their free will choices and who and what will assure their continuance.

"Not the large corporates and their owners?"

"Or the think tanks at those fine Universities whose very influential men and women meet and plan Strategies of the Future?"

"Of course, the shrinking tax paying public is not included in the deliberations of the future of globalism and its stated destruction of individual sovereignty – all behind heavy boardroom doors."

Also Johannes mentioned that the professional future of his colleagues and himself could not rely on the strategic objectives of career politicians and their lobbyists.

The team was reminded that former President Roosevelt once defined "Faschism" as the possession of a person, a group or another controlling power of a government, which excludes the people and its needs.

NPOs, large Foundations – Ford, Rockefeller - and their coveted tax free status influence the political landscape at the expense of the middle class.

Being "politically correct" means that the conventional wisdom should never be challenged.

This Ideology is fully permeated at the highest levels of corporate America: usually to exploit their own agendas, their smooth words of "our best days lie ahead" serve to disguise the real intention to create their brand of a "new slavery" under a more competitive environment.

The professors favored by the political elite designed new language to fit the Ideology; all regulators of the financial industry were included –SEC, FDIC, OCC, etc.

And, the new language or "speak" was designed to embellish the condition of the supervised entity; although the quality of the operation became increasingly suspect: the pool of cheap labor consisting of illegal immigrants and those not observing the visa rules became a tempting target of the political elite.

Johannes expected a high degree of organizational order at the top, however, recognized that the country was mired in the worst crisis ever.

The Crisis emanated from the negligent behavior of management and its avoidance of prudential credit and operational principles; decision making at the highest levels appeared to be unsatisfactory.

How could this be?

Johannes knew the answer.

At least 20 years in the making was this special kind of witches' brew; the cauldron was stirred constantly to a mighty froth.

Until the early 1980's Johannes and his team, as well as system wide, could conduct surprise visits – no announcements were necessary. Detailed review and audit work were conducted to determine compliance to best industry practices and its own internal guidelines.

While the external auditors provided a measure of comfort for the bank's board; their work procedures proved not optimal.

Federal Reserve work ethic and time spent to produce a detailed and reliable product with meaningful results and corrective actions was the standard to be followed by all regulators. And it was for many years.

While other regulators were periodically plagued by bank failures, the System, due to its stringent examination ethic demonstrated no failures.

Johannes sighed and asked aloud with his team why the major press and media always avoided the question: had the general relaxation of the former stricter examination ethic created the crisis?

Johannes remembered when the so-called Risk-Based Approach to examinations was introduced by the Board of Governors.

In its approach to becoming a **less-intrusive** examination unit, the not yet retired oracle expressed his pleasure at convincing the supervised institutions that the new approach was introduced by someone on neutral ground – a well -known professor at Columbia university.

Between 1995 and 1999, the team had to rely on various ad hoc procedures that replaced the voluminous manuals which were designed to thwart bank failures.

Prior to the professor's meeting with FRBNY management, Bill acquired a draft copy of the proposed reorganization of the BSG. It stressed the importance of a new Mantra.

"What in Hell is that?" said Johannes.

The board room gathering occurred in January of 2000.

Sitting front row in the prestigious board room were Alistair O'Bannon and Fernanda Buitoni, senior officers.

The rather portly professor stood squarely in front of his pulpit, and presented his thoughts.

The words began to flow smoothly out of his rounded mouth: "I think that this is the single most important change proposal I have reviewed for the BSG. As all in this room know, the world has been moving toward increased specialization for decades. As knowledge has expanded and finance has become more complex, Wall Street firms in the 1970s and large commercial banks in the 1980s virtually all decided that effectiveness requires specialization."

The pudgy professor strolled back and forth on the soft carpet, and emphasized that BSG urgently requires similar changes to keep up with its clientele.

"Unless the people who supervise and examine banks organize to use specialized skills and knowledge effectively, they will never be able to penetrate the increasingly sophisticated banks they are supposed to be regulating."

Alistair thought: who is this fat fuck that tells us how to do our job?!

Of course, he knew. He is a buddy of the current President of the FRBNY.

37

Fernanda thought otherwise.

She liked the issue of specialization and skill development, it diverted attention away from the real responsibility – be a tough regulator and save tax payer dollars by being always an opponent of negligent operations that ultimately bring a bank down.

"The advocates for this change want BSG to be more effective, that is, to produce more insightful examinations that help both the FRBNY and the banks being examined see risks more clearly. "

"Quality of outcomes drives this proposal."

Johannes thought: "I already don't like his professorial approach: he has not defined what he means by being **insightful**, and **how is quality of outcomes determined?**

And, he discusses **values.**

"In a role culture, the administrative end is valued. That is because in such a world positions are what matters, and getting each position to perform its designated task correctly is the essence of management."

Does he want us to become administrators? This dude is using college and textbook speak!

Are we now to focus on how well a report is written, instead of forcing a bank on the precipice of failure to get its act together?!

Then the dude pontificates further about a "task culture," the best written reports, and the development of the most skilled people leading to the best product.

"Well, he said it!"

"These assholes want us to spend our time with the process, not to rescue a bank from its "negligent and ineffective" operation!"

His voice began to sound like a drone. Heads in the audience began to nod, in approval or – when is this guy going to hurry up? I am going to miss my afternoon Starbucks!

Alistair and the team appeared to be in agreement that less time spent in writing up reviews of their colleagues would be more productive leaving more time for a deeper analysis of operational controls that lead to a financially stronger bank.

They would also resist the Fat Fuck's recommendation to have the banks being examined give a formal appraisal of both the examination process and, even more important, whether they have gained value from the report.

"Where did this guy get off?"

"We already know the risks!"

"The biggest one is whether they get paid back on time by the Borrower!"

"Also, when the staff doesn't follow established operations guidelines: strict segregation of front office from back office duties, concentration of loans and trading assets without proper approvals and booking, inadequate reserving of risk assets, lax audit staff and plan, and failure to comply with all applicable rules and regulations."

Johannes discussed the new system with the team, and all agreed that far less time would be devoted to ACTUAL examination work, too much time spent on the process, how to write reports, and valuable time allocated to the preparation work prior to an examination would act as a drag on the effectiveness of the team.

It would also revolve around the de facto phasing out of the thorough review of bank operations, and, the ultimate goal would be to phase out on-site work altogether!

Those not in agreement with the new order would be quietly ushered out the door – some with termination pay, others, considered long as "irredeemable" with little compensation. A slush fund for lawsuits would be set up.

The Other Terrorism

Johannes thought of the team, they had dispersed quickly, after Alistair and Fernanda showed their true colors. He did not know where they had gone. Their respective hiding places he also did not know. One day, they would come together stronger than ever.

The "Remnant Faithful" as we now can refer to the team, is ready to counter Satan's mentality of deep confusion and lack of understanding of the rules of time-proven Godly principles: the great gift of choosing a form of government that focuses on biblical principles.

They would re-group and perform once again their outstanding analysis of financial entities and bolster the overall integrity of the American financial system - on their terms, the application of righteous authority.

With this in mind, Johannes reflected on the "Sick Building Syndrome", many people have become slowly sickened with strange maladies brought on by vapor and unseen fumes. He wondered about the after effect of that day – the lingering unseen asbestos dust.

Also, the unseen particles circulating in the air globally in which the individual could not control. Of course few wanted to discuss this aspect of globalization. Few would dare challenge the conventional wisdom – it simply would not be politically correct to do so.

His management would simply shrug their shoulders and say "it is what it is."

Johannes observed the larger picture.

The major cities were succumbing to the attitude of "what me worry?"

The garbage in the inner cities were not being punctually picked up, small bits of paper food wrappers laid for days around the dumpsters, rotting food waste behind restaurants were an invitation for the rodents to enjoy their fare.

Was it true that more and more people suffered from lower back pain, and they could not or would not bend to pick up scraps of paper on the street? Did they not want to see their cities remain clean and orderly?

Were people really in that much of a hurry, to notice what was happening? Were they" multi-tasking" too much to notice the decline of pride in managing properly one's own Environment?

This new attitude became prevalent in the 1980's, it seemed that every corner of Society seemed to indicate that more and more, we became subjected to a life style of hurried efficiency.

Who of the Usual Suspects invented this idea of "Multi-tasking?"

Could this indirectly be part of the new Mantra expressed by that fat fuck?

Johannes began to understand that the Epoch of respectable bank supervision was about to disappear.

Too bad.

To criticize the new bank supervision system would bring from the disciples of this New Examination Methodology furrowed foreheads, odd facial expressions, raised eyebrows, and requests to come in to their office and discuss behind closed doors the essence of a better way to manage the supervised clients.

Such critical behavior, although necessary to isolate and correct areas that might be considered "opaque" if any, was frowned upon.

"Respectable Bank supervision" really meant, so the progressive, forward-looking Bank Supervisor of tomorrow, that no one person or system is perfect; rather, the more tolerant Managers would recognize and celebrate the cultural differences inherent in the center of a major city. Yes, even artistic wall and structural Graffiti represents societal diversity.

Alistair O'Bannon stood over six feet 5 inches tall, towered over most of his colleagues, wore typically medium striped suits, fashionable neck ties, English style black leather shoes, and a handkerchief in the left pocket of his coat.

He behaved like a King, a generous and fair type, treated his subjects with respect, and conveyed to his staff an attitude of confidence and calm.

As the Head of Bank Supervision, his office was no less imposing – fine digs, as others would say.

He could mingle with the important shareholders of large client banks. His confident demeanor and style of dress created openness with trust.

Johannes smiled, as he muttered "Lies have very short anchors."

One had to like this piece of shit. he loved the press people, he imagined to be a great leader and manager, as he folded his arms across his barrel –like chest, and his rather Caesar-like countenance indicated a readiness to be known as the leader of the Private Capital branch.

Alistair wanted all to know that he is "results oriented." He would sacrifice many to achieve the maximum return for an LBO.

He and his similarly dressed colleagues closed several non-competitive businesses, Grandma and Grandpa would no longer receive their Christmas gifts from the management because, well, these are now produced cheaper overseas!

It would be poor taste to continue this tradition as one could see the tiny gold colored paper stickers appended to each item as made in China!

Alistair's buddies wanted to establish a universal bank in the style of Citigroup and JP Morgan Chase. Their overseas units performed well.

His chums assured him that the interest shown by more and more shareholders and Fund owners continued to grow.

Alistair didn't trust this assessment since the Macroeconomic Indicators, such as Gross National product, National Income, interest rate fluctuations, consumer price index, retail trade, corporate profits, sometimes reacted otherwise!

Were they really familiar with the riskiness associated with the Investment banking business? They as members of the younger generation would like a certain proposal and immediately approve it. This attitude contributed to the "Robo-Signer" mentality, an offshoot of the politically correct culture.

These individuals practiced daily the art of correct speaking, and they would have to be respected, right?

The same people hesitated to differentiate between undocumented and illegally immigrated and individuals that followed strictly the immigration law to become citizens.

The usual suspects expressed their fucking know it all (FYA) opinion that the common menial tasks –yard work, picking agricultural produce, restaurant server, washing cars, and all was perceived as boring and mind numbing work.

The top boys and girls of the Chamber of Commerce, World Trade Organization, and the Corporate First Front (CFF) would have you believe that only the immigrant – especially the ones illegally in the country take the low paying jobs that the average citizen will no longer perform that type of work.

Utter nonsense, thought Johannes, since he as a student worked hard in the fields picking produce; the illegals only took their jobs away from them and the local underprivileged. Mowing lawns and working long hours as a bus boy in a restaurant were important sources of money to finance his education.

The CFF needed this new wave of illegal immigrants and other low paid job seekers to maximize their profits; decent paying jobs for the youth of America simply disappeared in favor of the new slavery.

Johannes explained to his staff of examiners that they soon, as members of the middle class, could become obsolete: the flood of illegal workers – those not observing the visa guidelines and sneaking across the border, as the CFF Elite and the major media heralded the message that as former colonialists we must somehow atone for our sins, and share our prosperity with the rest of the World-in reality the message was really "what is mine is yours!"

Or was the message the coming of a New World order?

Johannes remembered this day – September 3, 2001. Almost 2 years had passed since the Graham Bliley Act (GLB) became law by a complicit Congress and FRB Chairman, the Oracle, who desired to be less intrusive in the affairs of the banking system.

The Oracle and FRB Board of Governors, at the relentless insistence of the client banks, acquiesced. No more "surprise examinations!"

One of the most effective tools of any supervisory system is the ability to review AT ANY TIME the effectiveness of operational controls at the targeted entity.

This decision would prove to be a grave mistake. Unfortunately, other regulatory authorities quickly followed suit. They, too, wanted no "Agita."

Also, the practice of an extensive and detailed sample from all operational segments of an institution were scrapped in favor of a policy of risk identification and reliance on internal and external auditor reviews.

Rationale: not to repeat work already performed internally!

Johannes and his staff performed work in more detail and attention to accounting rules and their application, and extensive on-site discussions with operations to ascertain if work actually adhered to internal procedure – frequently the bank staff did not follow established procedure.

There began to be a long period of "pushback" against the

detailed work by Johannes and his team. Johannes sighed that their work would not be accepted again, and that past mistakes of bank management would be repeated and "lessons learned" completely ignored.

Meanwhile Johannes pushed the heavy barbell for 12 repetitions, and again. Bathed in sweat, he felt the Adrenalin rush through his body. His training partner watched him closely.

After work, visits to the health club enabled those of his team to release the built up tension of the day's examination work.

Johannes began to talk with himself, the others wondered what he was muttering.

Pearls of sweat began to roll down the middle of his muscular back, noticeable as he bent over to grasp the Olympic barbell to perform the deadlift – raising the heavy weight to his waist – 12 repetitions (reps), for three more times (sets) .

His lips moving rapidly: "the legacy, legacy systems." Again and again, as he strolled move toward the bench press rack.

He observed Johannes as he sat on the heavy bench, laid back and took the heavy barbell from the support, and let it sink slowly to his breast bone, then pushed it back over his head – the movement known as the "guillotine movement" for 15 repetitions. Five times he performed this exercise.

Super sets-more than 3 times the number of reps for each body part – biceps, triceps, upper back, legs, etc., and performed on a split routine basis-every other day, the upper body, etc.

After finishing the workout, he nodded to one of his colleagues, who respected Johannes because he wasn't an ass-kisser, used simple words to explain a point, not the confusing mish mash of a model analysis and difficult to understand math solutions, which, in reality, seldom came to pass.

The new examination technique rested on the principle of volatility occasioned by extreme price swings. The risk based analysis focused on volatility – financial market ups and downs.

While most of the team considered the university professor a windbag, FRBNY management's extraordinary talents were ignored – the elitist political environment had created a "paper tiger," an atmosphere of reluctant enforcement of tried and proven policies and procedures.

These assholes relied on the Political Correctness (PC) speak which basically sought to rule our lives.

The Era of a rigid writing style began with the acceptance of the GLB as Gospel for all regulatory agencies. A "Rules of the Road" manual reflecting the recommended writing style was distributed to every employee.

Johannes and his team would not accept this poppycock. Legacy was no more a riddle; the lessons learned from prior examinations showed the effectiveness of an aggressive and thorough methodology in which several stages of review with the examined entity's staff, their documentation, and separation of duties from management were supported in private by the Oracle.

However, publicly, the Oracle did not pay attention to the prior bank supervision methodology. Instead, he indicated that his view would be that the Financial System could be self-supervising, and the new Role of the FRB would be as an "Umbrella" supervisor.

His colleague stated further that "few people have as much confidence in the self-supervision of the financial children than

Mr. Greenspan." Johannes muttered, "Yes about as certain as the Amen in the Church."

With these important questions about the new system, and how effectively it could be executed, his thoughts were interrupted by the events of September 11, 2001.

He remembered well that morning when he, around 8:20 a.m., bought his organic pastry from his favorite local farmer at the bottom of Tower #2. Tuesdays and Thursdays the local farmers always offered their baked goods and produce.

This particular morning was very easy to describe – the air was crisp and cool, sunny and not so warm. The streets were clean of refuse and materials typically left behind by crowds of tourists.

On the southeast side of the street he was within 50 yards of the Twin Towers of the World Trade Center. For several months Johannes purchased these wonderful tasting pastries as he exited his commuter bus which regularly brought him into the Wall Street district.

He enjoyed looking up at these magnificent Buildings, their ultimate height on foggy mornings was obscured, even on sunny days, one had to stand back a few feet to marvel at the engineering feat, the tallest in the world for a time.

On this day, he met that German attorney who met him at the foot of Liberty Street. He had just arrived from Frankfurt. He had never before visited the city.

Together, they walked to the office. During the short walk, they spoke in the German language.

He was so pleased that an American used his Mother Tongue and this made him more comfortable in a strange city. Also, he had another reason which at times bothered him that so many in Germany preferred to speak English rather than their native tongue.

They shared the same opinion that the banking industry and other business people within the European Union (EU) used the English language excessively. They agreed: as if America and England ruled the world!

Hard to believe?

No, thought Johannes because the large American banks preferred to conduct their business in English and anyone that preferred another language would be looked at as if this was somehow un-American.

Johannes said "Yes, I remember this jerk, Ron was his first name, a national banker with the California bank that I used to be associated with, and he with his other local university colleagues who graduated with him, admitted foolishly that one does not need to learn other languages since everyone in the world would speak English."

"He became more of a jerk because he criticized others that had other language capabilities because they did not seem to be American enough to properly represent the interests of an American bank when they were dealing with foreign bankers."

"And the management of this extremely conservative California bank even believed this envy-oriented crap that Ron spewed out."

The man from Frankfurt nodded politely and smiled. Johannes continued: "Not surprising since one can really sense the superiority of these men in their dark suits, white shirts and striped ties when one steps unto the 26th floor. In this group there were no women.

The man from Frankfurt smiled and said: "Yes, Mr. Emmerich, it is difficult to accept, although one could only see this on television – perhaps a television series like Dallas." Yes, they both agreed.

They arrived within 100 meters of the Maiden Lane office building which stood opposite the fort-like structure of the Federal Reserve Bank of New York.

Around 8:35 a.m. they entered the building and took the elevator to the 23rd floor. They waited a few seconds before the fine polished stainless steel doors of the elevator finally opened. As they stepped into the hallway, they saw the name plates of the officers of Bank Supervision.

At that time, Johannes was not clear as to how these personalities would become a burden to his future life.

He went to the glass double-doors, entered his ID card into the reader, the door clicked open and Johannes and Joerg strolled through the doors to Johannes's work area.

The area contained a large window through which one could see both towers of the famous World Trade Center, whose arrogant and splendid form pierced the blue sky. The morning sun gleamed prominently on this modern-day Tower of Babel.

Unknown to us, on this day, the fragile man-made idolatry would soon be nothing more than rubble. Like the Tower of Babel, nothing lasts forever.

To others, the WTC signified a hated example of the arrogance of a form of corrupt capitalism.

This once gleaming aluminum and glass structure would implode and create a huge hole in the ground and a gigantic smoke plume would provide not only toxic dust but, for the curious and the ones that always had to look at tragedy, it simultaneously became a horrendous atmosphere of sadness.

Alistair, on this day, wore particular colors which became emblematic of various shades of gold and green – somewhat psychological in nature, according to him. It reminded Johannes of one of his economics professors who also wore a gold shirt and as he waved his arms about to make a point one could see the perspiration rolling down his shirt.

Alistair's face revealed few wrinkles, showed a very strong forehead, which was partly covered by a not too thin patch of golden brown hair.

Many say that no one could speak ill of him since he knew all of the corners and angles inherent in a career spent in the Federal Reserve System because he held all of the reigns in his hands.

On this tragic day, Alistair appeared more than relaxed – even victorious.

The echo of the first plane striking the North Tower sounded like steel pipes falling on the street below.

Alistair stood up, ran to the window and looked at the North Tower and saw what appeared to be the 101st floor disintegrate into shreds of aluminum strips which once was part of the top façade of the tower.

He could also see the enormous hole created by the attack plane and paper confetti appeared suspended in the air trying to escape the black and red flames licking out of the tower hoping to find its objective.

Obviously, there was no "ticker tape" parade below.

This Picture Doesn't Hang Straight

Alistair quickly moved from the window but one could still see the imprint of his face formed by his heavy breathing.

He suddenly heard sobbing and screaming which came from the Board Room across his office.

He saw his colleagues watching the gruesome scenes - terror stricken looks of despair on the faces of jumping employees of the once prestigious investment firm, Cantor Fitzgerald.

They had no chances of survival.

Below, Johannes witnessed the cascading bodies bouncing off the North Tower, the office memos and marketing reports spewed out of the flames engulfed windows, the shredded confetti lasted at least an hour.

The former Bankers Trust tower stood majestically next to the yet to be struck South tower. Many of Johannes' colleagues were conducting a detailed review of the now Deutsche Bank owned institution.

Despite the stress and pressure of the situation, his face still showed relaxed concern. Perhaps the Monarch would have an escape plan in his mind.

Strange, thought Johannes.

Sometime later Johannes would better understand that facial expression of his boss.

His concern about the events of the day exhibited something else, something entirely different.

It said a lot about the real Alistair. What was he thinking? After the collapse of the North Tower, it was not possible to enjoy a look out of the window as the brown toxic dust enveloped everything. On this side of the Maiden Lane building it seemed that for a few moments night had fallen.

Opposite Johannes and Joerg one could hear Fernanda scream "away, away – leave everything behind! Run, run!"

Johannes and Joerg noticed that she, an executive vice president of the entire Federal Reserve Bank of New York had real panic in her voice; computers, files, confidential data, personal effects, lunch remains still on desks, everything was left behind by the panic-stricken officers and examination employees.

The decision to leave everything behind and save oneself was viewed at first as very clever but this decision on her part proved to be reckless.

Nobody had any inkling how cowardly the management would behave in the coming weeks.

Alistair walked slowly through the white painted hallway until he reached the stairs. He moved his head right and left before he went down the stairs.

Suddenly, the power to the entire building was turned off, so the toxic brown dust could no longer come into the building via the air conditioning systems.

The air became acrid and still. Sweating became the norm for everyone. Soon the clothing on the more corpulent bodies began to show sweat marks, no one had to time to look at the more attractive women whose soaked blouses reflected the best that our Creator gave, perhaps Adam and Eve types?

Johannes said to Joerg and the others "let's follow Alistair down the stairs." Johannes looked at Joerg and noticed his military-type of walking as he went through the emergency door.

The emergency staircase was dark; nobody had a flashlight. Each person negotiated the concrete steps carefully, this was no time for falling and injuring knee caps.

Finally, a woman carrying a flashlight met us on the 15th floor and showed us the way down. We hastened down the remaining steps.

Once outside, we could now breathe the air, before the South Tower collapsed just seconds after leaving the maiden Lane office tower.

A similar deafening to the ears explosion caused one to look up and see the upper portion of the building tilt to the left – identical to the collapse of the North Tower, before the entire building caved in and created a huge tidal wave of debris.

Within seconds before reaching the main building, some 20 meters away, we became snowmen. It was not immediately obvious to us that we were covered in white dust.

Inside, we placed protective masks over our noses and mouths because the air conditioning system continued to suck in the toxic dust. The system's reverberation seemed labored as the dust seemed to clog the ventilation ducts, and the dust began to seep in and cloud the overhead lighting.

This situation lasted for an hour. There was no seating. Some even sat on the floor. The signal towers for cell phone operation were not functioning. The terror stricken sobbing began again - the thought of not surviving this day became very real.

There were angry shouts of some kind of retribution against

those responsible for the collapse of the towers. The two gigantic holes in the ground emitted black plumes of smoke for days.

After several hours the management informed us that we should go home.

We left the building and trudged through a snowfield of toxic dust which covered our feet up to our ankles in order to walk to the subway and take the trains to our respective destinations.

The laptops became heavier and heavier as Johannes and Robert Lancia, his internal auditor examiner, trudged further through the toxic dust.

Many people wore the terror of the day on their faces, and turned into wild animals forcing themselves in to any form of public transport.

Johannes and Robert chose the more difficult way of escape – shoe leather express.

Johannes wondered how many of the team would be available to continue their work.

Fortunately, all escaped. They did not listen to the reassuring voices of the Port of Authority on loud speakers stating all to remain in their places as help would soon be on its way.

"Bullshit, I'm out ta here!!," responded some of the team, who left the South Tower just in time; running down 85 flights of stairs before the second Tower was struck by another plane. Breathless and sweating profusely, they ran in all directions. Mere seconds separated these stalwart men and women from certain death and life.

THIS PICTURE DOESN'T HANG STRAIGHT

Of course, the public officials would proclaim the area to be safe from toxic materials. Wrong!

The blueprints of the buildings that were constructed and completed in in 1970 indicated otherwise – asbestos was a major material used; and, perhaps tons of toxic dust and debris lay on the ground initially before strong winds would carry the microscopic debris in many directions.

Also, the Bankers Trust tower became a "white Elephant" no longer safe to enter the building as the devastating impact of the destruction had weakened the foundation.

A perfect opportunity for thieves to enter by night and steal anything and everything, all FRBNY laptops were missing, according to FRBNY management. How much confidential information became known to others, could not be determined.

Also the media did not disclose the presence of many dump trucks removing metal debris that could later be sold in the black market.

In the meantime, Joerg took up temporary residence in one of the mid-town hotels; the strenuous hours during the collapse of the WTC had taken its toll of his physical energy. He was worn out.

He tried to call Johannes the next morning, but it was not easy to reach him, since the communications network had been under pressure during and after the attacks, and it would be many hours before top management would pull their heads out of their asses.

Management had set up an 800 number in case of emergencies. But no one could imagine that management now required that previously delegated persons must have access to their personal computers to effect communications.

57

"Hello, hello!!" Like duty-conscious soldiers, that must be able to obey orders from the Chief Officer, and the personnel discovered how 'battle ready" they really were!

Now some began to remember the panicky outbursts from Fernanda: "Run, run, leave everything behind!"

Johannes remembered this embarrassing situation, and how relaxed Alistair appeared, he even smiled as he was reminding others to be careful in their descent down the building stairs.

It was completely unknown to Johannes, his team, and other staff the brand of the new irradiation machines that were quickly brought in and stationed before all entrances and exits of the Central Bank and its satellite office buildings.

The Installation of these customized machines occurred only two days after the collapse of the WTC and its adjacent buildings in the Plaza.

According to the security Guards these new irradiators could render anything perishable totally useless, even the tiny spores of anthrax bacteria!

Some weeks before, Alistair was enjoying a cup of his favorite brand of coffee in the main building cafeteria, when he heard a rather gruff voice call out his name: "Awwlistaaar is that yeeew?"

Laughing lustily: "Yeeew loooouuk deeeeep in sumpthin!"

Alistair whirled around quickly to shake hands with his old buddy of the university days. Alfred strolled over to his table, his gait rocked side to side, a spinal distortion was the cause. He wore a size 14 shoe, stood over 6' 7" tall, but rather lean appearing in his Dickies overalls.

Alfred was the President of Secure Systems (SS), the largest manufacturer and marketer of irradiation equipment and spare parts. He drawled further about Alistair's idea, as he reached for a partly used paper napkin, and began to draw with a partly chewed off pencil the concept.

He noticed others in the cafeteria looking at him and he endeavored to speak more clearly, shrugging off the folksy accent, and said: "of course, we have a chance not only to feed a hungry world, eliminate hunger, but we have a huge opportunity to rake in the Bucks!"

He continued: "we must set up a type of industrial Oligarchy. And we would be questioned by interested parties – financial analysts, potential investors, and so forth, how and for what purpose."

"The key rests in the continuation of our propaganda, and our lobbyists would be supportive, over the absolute Necessity of adequate food safety. First we have to convince the public that our technology is indispensable to adequate food safety and supply worldwide!!"

Alistair dreamed of irradiating all foods for the astronauts in space; we must have that contract! Also the armed services.

"Second, our lobbyists must convey to the right governmental persons our message so that our concept is fully accepted and supported. After their formal acceptance, we then will have the most influential governmental voices in our pockets!"

"Third, we will arrange several press conferences, whose objective is to fully explain to the public the concept and its many advantages and few negatives with the technology. Also, the favorable results of many years of testing would be disclosed."

During some of the press meetings, Alistair stood in the back part of the room and thought of hiring a contractor that was owned by a large hedge fund. A large contract between SS and this fund would not be out of the question, since the former Treasurer of the US was a close friend.

He conjured up a multi-billion US dollar contract, which gave them complete rights to install in every Post Office and relevant government buildings the irradiators!

Johannes learned later that the US postal service had already invested in these irradiators. Alistair bragged that within seconds his machines would kill off the feared anthrax bacteria. All correspondence destined for Washington DC would have to pass through these machines prior to delivery to the recipient.

Alfred and Alistair Anthrax did their homework. An infection is the result of exposure to this germ and appears in grazing animals and humans.

If enough anthrax dust is inhaled into the lungs, it can cause inhalation anthrax, the deadliest form of the disease, and the toxic buildup can cause problems and lead quickly to death!

The contractor firm and SS were now in discussions with a European life insurance company for a mix of bond and stock private placement. Once fully placed, Alistair would harvest several million US dollars. Not bad he mused.

Through future transactions, he would earn millions! This prospect provided him a real Reason to celebrate! Besides he would ride the wave of perceived population growth, more potential customers, then more wheeling and dealing! He mused: "it is good to be me!"

Johannes did not then know what the irradiators could do and what they indeed were. He decided to look more deeply in to this unfamiliar (to him) area of food safety.

But he did remember a demonstration on Wall street a few weeks ago by individuals wearing short sleeved cotton shirts which front side read: "The Department of Energy has a solution to the problem of radioactive waste. You are going to eat it!"

The T-shirt also exhibited a huge mushroom cloud (from a nuclear blast) over a plate of foodstuffs. Underneath:

"Your help is needed to stop Food Irradiation." A 1 800 phone number also followed.

Johannes wondered, what in the Hell did all that mean?

He decided to find out more about this methodology claimed by the government to be safe in use without serious side effects.

The demonstrators appeared to be average middle class adults, not the Hippie types so much associated with health foods, organic foods, etc.

Johannes would soon be able to link Alistair's business strategy with those business plans of Big Pharma, allegedly designed to heal the wealthy at the expense of the lesser income groups.

Alistair knew that the advice of Pasteur had long been ignored; Big Pharma took the easy way out: enhance shareholder value through the steady introduction of new medications, and facilitate rapid approval by the government authorities, in order to accelerate cash flow.

The chance of quick profit rested on insider purchases prior to regulatory approval of any new medication. Alistair took advantage of the poor management style of the bureaucracy.

Of course, one should take heed to execute insider trades carefully. A good example would be the case of a former FDA Head, who appeared before the Judge to learn about her sentencing in court on February 2007.

The former FDA Chief was fined US $ 90,000 and must serve a three year sentence of supervised activity: no trading of securities related to Big Pharma.

It was unclear why he had left his post two months after his confirmation by the US Senate. Of course, he lied about his extensive trading of food processing and drug company securities due to his "insider" knowledge of the firms' future activities.

His attorney had defended him earlier that his infringement of the ethics rules was not deceptive or fraudulent!

Johannes and the team had discussed this case for hours, and questioned when "enough is enough."

These lawbreakers were the real impetus behind the financial crises and manufactured volatility. The issue of "unjust enrichment" is also clearly portrayed in the relationship between medical doctors (MD) and representatives of Big Pharma. According to file information, a recent survey disclosed that four of five MD's accept dinners and expensive alcoholic beverages from Drug companies.

"Wow!" exclaimed Bill as he continued to leaf through the huge credit file of one of the largest drug firms. He turned to another Article that appeared in a major city newspaper in April, 2007. It covered a Survey of testing various drug products, the participants would receive certain fees for their comments as well as all other costs incurred for the survey.

The overall strategy of Big Pharma and their doctors was to re-classify as normal health issues the discovery of new sicknesses, tumors, lack of sexual desire, perceived change of life problems and others to portray a normal life for healthy individuals. Subtle marketing tricks would show that an otherwise healthy person must have these newer drugs, etc. to maintain good health!

However, the file did indicate that several diagnoses of conditions were exaggerated or totally wrong, especially for cases of ADHD, even some noted pediatric and neurologic physicians considered the diagnoses as a 100 percent swindle!

Even the FDA became concerned over the number of suicides and attempted suicides between years 1982-2000. A widely prescribed medication for Acne to millions of patients was viewed to be problematic for the nervous system!

"Big Pharma promises Health, but, of course its entire business depends on the spread of sickness." Bill echoed further class action lawsuits against other suspect drugs.

The next credit officer's memo in the file stirred up Bill even more. The National Institutes of Health (NIH) conducted a study on the effectiveness of the multi-billion dollar chemotherapy application to treat cancer, and found that alternatives like food supplements and high doses of specific vitamins were more affordable, safer, and yielded good outcomes.

Further: to counter the negative result of the NIH report, Big Pharma became the largest financial contributor in election campaigns. Its task: continue the Hoax. The charade is easy to assure, since there are six lobbyists per one member of Congress, and many of these are former Representatives and Senators.

Johannes thought about a recent statement by Management Guru Peter Drucker: "the Greed and Avarice of corporate management will lead to America's decline in economic leadership worldwide."

Johannes wondered if the New World Order (NWO) idea was still in vogue?

The NOW, referred often as the new feudalism comes from that Dynasty, which propagates this idea, which is not new.

Twenty years ago Presidents Reagan and Bush introduced a newer concept: the maximum freedom of human expression without significant oversight.

Yes, as long as someone profits from it. Johannes remembered someone else that was very familiar with this concept: 32nd president of the US, Franklin Delano Roosevelt (FDR).

A recent visit with some of the analyst staff at the BOG would last two days, with some time off for visiting the many historical sites of the nation's capital. On this occasion, he visited FDR's monument.

Johannes remembered one quote in particular, in so many words, it meant that a government that permits a few men to name their system as a NWO, is not new and it is no Order.

Further, the promise of the American dream does not mean uncontrolled capitalism as in the days of Charles Dickens.

The "FEW" or those "usual suspects" have not really changed their MO over the years; today the Few feel very comfortable pursuing their unsavory ideas, since most watch the "tube" too much, therefore can be manipulated easily, especially by unscrupulous college professors preaching their own brand of political elitism, which, like the NOW concept, is not new.

The American chamber of commerce and other special interest groups have on their payroll numerous lobbyists and agitators to spread their message of 'cheap labor" to perform the jobs that citizens allegedly will no longer perform.

Johannes thought; yes, as long as the world continues to turn, the same actors will be on stage.

Johannes and the team asked themselves often: "how long must we continue to swallow this crap?"

"Excuse me, we are still being taken to the cleaners!"

Other comments were uttered that tended to border on the obscene, especially in the presence of the female team members.

The usual suspects reveled in their new found deregulated environment, or was it the lack of enforcement of existing regulations that brought on so much glee?

The team witnessed the new "Smoke and mirrors" environment, since this behavior enjoyed the friendly Approval of the NOW.

The result of the new order was not positive: the Asset Strippers had really fucked the middle class, stolen their money, and wanted their Soul! The team began to witness the dissolution of one of the most sacred achievements of the middle class – the pension.

Johannes: "The asset strippers, bless their little hearts, wanted their elitist pols to extend the Social Security (SS) retirement age from 67 to 72 years of contributed service. And, they pushed hard for a re-classification of the SS program to an entitlement!"

Bullshit!

Of course the worker made contributions via taxation to support future withdrawals, and now, the elitists backed their cronies in Congress to borrow from the SS Fund to finance general government expenses – another expression for outright theft from the future recipients. This new terrorism became global.

The non-enforcement of existing regulations designed to protect all depositors, asset holders, investors, labor union members, retirees, widows, and so forth gained more momentum, since the clever politicians and their elitist new order pushed their agenda.

What this really means is that the voters no longer have the "Say" regarding their own welfare: wages, taxation, business opportunity, outsourcing of jobs to low wage countries, financial institution stability, instead these decisions are made by a cadre of unelected bureaucrats, tax favored institutions, and corporate lobbyists.

Globally the losers are everywhere as the lion's share of daily increasing income remains at the top. The Corporate Front First (CFF) – whose members form the leadership of most countries, is more powerful than the world Trade Organization (WTO).

Main Strategy of the CFF: alignment of all wages in developed countries to balance out those of the under developed countries so that the primary objective – annually increasing Shareholder Value, continues to be satisfied.

Johannes mulled over the situation, and remembered the historically accurate gladiator games of ancient Rome, and the fallen fighter depended on the direction of the Caesarian (up or down) thumb – most of the time, the fate of the fallen gladiator did not augur well.

Tantamount to begging, the shrinking middle class of developed countries must be content with declining overall compensation in the near future.

Law and other Alternatives

When Johannes completed his graduate University education, he remembered the hard times, which provided him nothing more than serious concern about the timing of securing the job of his choice.

At that time, he had really good luck. The year was 1973, and the first oil embargo had just gone into effect. Prices at the pump had suddenly risen from twenty cents to US One dollar a gallon.

The worst economy which his generation had ever experienced, scarcely offered a person good work opportunities, because they not only had to accept very negative work conditions, but endure the stressful situations with their parents, which normally offered financial support to their children.

Unfortunately during this time a significant number of parents had already lost their work positions in the last year.

The reduced chances to secure middle class work forced many to hold down more than one job.

Oh, yes.

The blessings of competitive economic conditions based on free market principles!

Johannes wondered who had designed the basis of a free market.

Was this concept invented by the influential men and women of this country?

Or perhaps one could polish the shoes of the "Top Boys and Girls", and earn good tip money!

While man has upset the Equilibrium of Nature, so it must be with the financial world!

Johannes also reasoned that the large companies would have the opportunity to exploit global resources, and the finance industry with their regulators could have free rein over the public market place.

The scavengers of yesterday are the same animals of today.

Nothing has changed. Life remains unfair. Johannes knew this in his earlier adventures in the work place.

The Asset Strippers during the 1970's dressed conservatively, did not wear "flashy" garb, so as not to attract the attention of vengeful former employees of bankrupt or poorly managed companies falling prey to the wolves of the financial world.

He mused: or I could perform the worthy work of a "Bag Boy" for the Wall Street Executives! And I could own a fancy cell phone, and take pictures of the top boys and girls with the built in camera.

And the drugs were not pharmaceutical grade, but they provided the wealthy consumer a certain enjoyment of a 'high."

Johannes observed the daily machinations of the New York Jungle which offered more and more jobs of lesser quality.

In those earlier days of innovative financial instruments offered by the Bankers Trust Company, Johannes attended these sessions, and the journalists of the usual suspect news organizations appeared to show interest of a rapturous nature.

The theoretical advantages of these instruments did not fit well with existing Reality: Good and evil people, free movement of capital, toxic drug consumption, increasing crime, and the avalanche of cheap imported goods.

It was easy for Johannes to determine the purpose of this Mess. He realized that the "Multis" ruled everything!

And the banks financed everything possible under the guise of "general corporate purposes" or one could also believe that they created financial terrorism!

Idealism of free markets would overcome most obstacles, as they told the media, which they controlled!

Man, what is going on? Only a very few individuals could play this new game.

During the Reagan, Clinton and Bush years the middle class would find that it was becoming more and more irrelevant to the new strategy.

The new migrants to the large cities seeking work emanated from the farms because of lower land prices and income from the agricultural production.

The bright lights of the big cities attracted many searching for the big opportunity, which for some never came. The new labor market entrants would soon find out about the "dog eat dog" environment inherent in the big city.

Too much power, influence, and wealth in the hands of the few created a myriad of problems and threatened to destroy our America, thought Johannes.

Unbridled greed has been around for a long time. If only people would learn how to live and get along with one another!

The most revered book in the world provided the solution: love me with all your heart and follow my commandments, and love others as you would love yourself.

Simple. If only people would adhere to these rules.

"God's warning to us was very clear," said Johannes to his Remnant Faithful.

The once standing World Trade Center was now a pile of human and material pieces which one could never piece together again.

Johannes knew that Epoch of hubris filled men and women strutting their stuff, was now over.

Other plunderers in the dead of night would take their fair share of the most valuable of scrap metal, and no one allegedly saw what was going on.

The sons and daughters born at the end of World War II would be dammed to disaster because of their parents' constant focus on luxury and other worldly pleasures.

The good old times and the years of excessive plenty were best demonstrated by the many Cadillacs and Lincolns in the garages of the new rich – the oil men, and the readiness of this new influential class to show the rest of the world how to behave, ignited the fuse of the financial terrorism Dynamite!

ADRIAN VOGT

The unbridled power of financial managers and their regulators led to a comfortable attitude of turning their nose upward to the people that needed to borrow, especially this class- the now almost extinct middle class.

Bill laughed, and said: "The greatest fuckup of all time is now fermenting in a champagne bottle that is almost empty."

"Without effective oversight, financial terrorism is in full swing!"

The clever people could see the crisis coming.

Now, the experts were scrambling to invent a reason(s) for the brewing storm. They became desperate to find a reason, anything, because the average person was dumb or didn't quite think things through to the end.

"The main reason is the human inclination to swing from fear to extreme euphoria, not the principles of capitalism!"

"No economic Paradigm can suppress this inclination, without exacting heavy, heavy damage to the overall economy!"

Here comes the clincher, thought Bill.

The Oracle pursed his lips, and quietly said: "Regulation, alleged to be an effective solution for the current crisis, was never historically capable of preventing or eliminating financial crises!"

Johannes and the others could hardly believe what they were hearing from the former Chairman of the Board of Governors of the Federal Reserve System.

It should be no surprise that so many scholarly types were out of touch with reality.

The team recognized also that these types continued to cover up their inability to separate fact from fiction.

When the current crisis broke out, one assumed that the weak link in the chain was the unregulated Hedge Funds and Private Capital.

But the mounting losses occurred at the strongest regulated institutions – the money center banks.

The memory of these events continued to haunt Johannes.

The team believed stricter conduct of established Examination guidelines during the last twenty years would have prevented the savings and loan (S&L) and sub-prime crises.

Johannes voiced the opinion of the group in this manner: "after several investigations and review of the S&L crisis in 1989, we came to the conclsion that the real enemies were the top decision makers with the responsible state and federal regulators who hindered intentionally the reporting of well known problems at the time that were clearly spelled out – grossly negligent credit policies at most S&Ls."

"Further, instead of a clearly illustrated warning of the growing credit crisis, the top managers hid the findings of field examiner reports, which accurately described the deficient financial situation of the S&Ls, in their desk drawers!"

"And several examples of non adherence to internal guidelines of the regulators existed."

In early September 2008, a report by the Justice Department, indicated the resignation of the former Security Adviser to President Clinton, since this person had taken classified information to his residence without approval of the custodian of Classified and Confidential documents.

Hard to explain was the destruction of three of the five documents taken, these were stuffed in to his suit pocket, some in his pants and socks, as he left the building.

This Official claimed to have inadvertently or mistakenly taking these items!

In the interim, these documents were hidden at a construction site outside the building, and he later took these to his home.

Documents taken included handwritten notes that contained warnings by the secret service of impending terror attacks before or after the year 2000.

Other media reports indicated the cover up of details of the Investigatory Commission that affected politicians and business leaders.

The suppression of the impending worsening situation could have been addressed and resolved by responsible government authorities.

Johannes thought along with the team, that the looser supervision through risk focused supervision became the model for all government entities!

Or, more seriously, were the perpetrators trying to rewrite history in their favor!?

Also the same careless supervision of classified documentation and followup procedures led to the so-called risk focused examinations of supervised institutions which ultimately resulted in the non-disclosure of numerous operations problems and the absence of strict comprehensive sampling of risk assets.

The GLB not only encouraged a less rigorous examination atmosphere but relied heavily on the dynamics of home and securities markets prices under competitive conditions.

The Oracle exercised his beautiful word language by emphasizing the dynamic nature of home and common stock share prices and the acceptance of such, and "we have to resist every call to limit the competitiveness of capital markets!"

"The noticeably strong performance of the world economy prior to the financial crisis, indicates an importance acceptance of the flexibility of free markets, and the necessity of sufficient equity in the mortgage backed securities markets!"

The faces of Johannes and the team looked bewildered, since the so called financial experts seemed to seldom ask the right questions!

These questions would point to the importance of viable collateral, ability of the borrower to repay the loan on time, and supporting documents evidencing these criteria.

Of course, it did not matter to the finance terrorists and their zeal to place securities with mortgage collateral and just enough documentation to satisfy the rating agencies and the end investor.

In the strategy of the usual suspects, the ultimate repayment source would be the tax payer, since the fear of a "Great Depression" would dominate most people's thinking.

The temptation of enormous fees for the placement of the mortgages in various tranches rated investment grade was too great to spend much time on the mundane task of the validation of repayment source.

Johannes and the team members enjoyed reminiscing about their prior experiences in the industry, in particular those during 1985.

These ranged from overseas to local bank officer positions and the accepted conservative credit approval and repayment practices.

They also discussed the early days of the leveraged buyout, in particular, the Wometco transaction, a Miami, Florida cable TV enterprise introduced by certain Officers of the former Continental Bank and Trust, Chicago, Illinois.

Johannes had always suspected the motives of the fine dressed LBO Kings and Queens, who would not hesitate to look at you in a strange manner if one asked too many questions about this new financing.

They wanted all bankers to be convinced that the LBO was the wave of the future to promote corporate managerial efficiency.

What did that mean?

Bill and Susan both questioned in their own thoughts whether this new financing portended more debt in the finance markets based on, they would soon find out, narrow cash flow to debt servicing ratios, some transactions at a 1: 1 ratio – one dollar of debt to be paid by one dollar of cash flow from operations.

Does this sound familiar? The Sting of a potential Fraud?

Yes!

These former Officers of the defunct Continental Illinois Bank, loved to socialize, promote global Capitalism, their home is the global market place, and they resented criticism of their ideas.

They knew best for the world, since they represented a strong cross section of the CFF!

Besides, they are – in their own eyes, very important people.

Also brought into the discussion of the LBO, was Alischraga, the devoted wife of Johannes. She became very upset about this new development in the market place: "How can these people sleep at night? Because of the mass layoffs, which ultimately result as a means to finance an LBO."

In agreement, Johannes raised his voice: "the management and the financing team shop at the finest shoe stores, purchase their Bruno Magli shoes, while the laid off employees struggle to put bread and milk on their table."

The monetary proceeds of an LBO really create problems for so many families of the now unemployed staff and operations, as recognized by the Credit Department of a bank in Frankfurt, Germany, that Johannes had been with for several years.

The LBO, according to the Director of the Credit Department, contained a lot of air, little substance, because of the very large debt burden to finance the existing management's sale of the company to the new investors – the initiators of the LBO.

Important questions: where does the future cash flow emanate? Are there liquidity issues? Is the repayment of the huge debt burden feasible?

The regulators became concerned and promulgated various guidelines to examine the LBO and endeavor to control the excessive leverage a bank might have to take on its own books.

For a while, due to the S&L crisis in 1988/89, the LBO came in disfavor, when the potential negative consequences came to light: the ultimate takeout for the debt burden would be the sale of various parts of the company in the capital markets, if the conditions were right – no recession or economic problems to deal with.

The headlines of some newspapers did not augur well for the LBO investor: "the American tax payer must "ante up" more money!"

Johannes was not pleased as he read an article dated July 2008, that quoted the experts as saying this debacle could not occur again, but anything was possible!

The team was buzzing like a beehive of agitated bees, as they came to the conclusion that some regulators were the problem, that the government too willingly bailed out the firms responsible for the crisis. Government agencies competing against the private mortgage finance market caused it to dry out – liquidity became almost non-existent.

This was not a good picture. It hung crooked on the wall, so to speak. It might take some time to re-align the picture.

Johannes' hands shook as he read further: "Shareholders take a beating. Sunny reports of investment firms could not be believed as they were part of the problem due to the excessive marketing of derivative products that promised an assured takeout for the purchaser of credit default protection."

He wondered if the situation for the investor was really better than in the last five or ten years?

He chuckled as he heard Bill say: "would you hire this type to manage your own portfolio?"

What happened to the excessive fee income charged for credit protection? A key question posed to the group by Susan.

A heated discussion among the team ensued: "How was the fee income booked? As an immediate credit to revenue, or was this revenue matched with the expense over a period of years as credit protection might endure longer than one year?"

She continued: "would one think that the wise bankers and their conservative capital backers could offer these so called innovative solutions like the CDO's and the CLO's to clever bankers in other countries?"

Johannes noticed a sarcastic tone in Susan's voice.

"Because the Regulators hadn't conducted their work properly?"

"Or the supervisory work would be too intrusive for these new customers of the Regulators, naturally we would want all of our customers to earn sufficient money!"

Johannes left the area and returned home for the day. His lovely wife greeted him at the door. She took his hand, and said: "enough for today. I know that your work can be very demanding and frustrating. Let's rest, in bed."

She let her green Sari drop to the floor. She was totally naked. She climbed in bed and laid on the silken sheets. He laid next to her. And they caressed themselves for at least twenty minutes, before they fully satisfied their respective physical appetites.

They beamed with joy. They enjoyed this type of sport. One lives for the other.

Alischraga thought of her marriage as ideal; they functioned as partner, friend and lovers. They shared common interests in the kitchen and concentrated on the Art of Cooking. After a meal of sweet breads (calves pancreas), previously marinated with red wine, and combined with roasted potatoes in a mixture of spices from the middle east, they ate their vanilla yogurt for dessert.

Afterwards they leaned back in their chairs and looked at each other for a few minutes. Then Alischraga nodded her head affirmatively and cleared the table. She took the sponge from the edge of the kitchen sink and wiped the table and place mats clean.

Then she removed her apron and folded it neatly and laid it on the counter top and sat down on the black leather couch. She slipped her feet out of the fine leather flats and rested her feet on the hand- made leather foot stool, which they purchased in Morocco. Her well-formed toes were always painted with deep red nail polish.

She then pulled the seam of her emerald green Sari slightly back so she could determine if the black hair on her shapely legs was too long. Her Johannes liked the complete woman, attractive and sensual, as Nature intended.

Johannes strolled in to the family room, and greeted her respectfully. She sighed: "I am quite tired, please go about your work."

She thought deeply about her relationship with him, she had found a new happiness, she knew also that a happy marriage can only endure with a deep respect for one another, she is very proud of him, as this thought caused tears of joy that began to veil over her beautiful deep dark eyes.

She shared his thoughts of the dangers of globalism and the complete loss of individual sovereignty.

THIS PICTURE DOESN'T HANG STRAIGHT

A balanced life would be more and more difficult to achieve as long as the new terrorism existed: the continued worship of the false gods of the global corporate and government elite and the subsequent loss of respect for God's commandments.

"You are right, Johannes, but what are we able to do against the evil trying to conquer our beloved land?"

Johannes became silent, but he had a plan.

Incompetence and Short Term Gain

Jonathan Swift, the English-Irish Author, was one of Johannes' favorite writers. He had imagination!

One quote which lodged firmly in his head was: "A wise man keeps his money in his head, but not in the heart!"

The securities markets recovery from the depths of the 2008/2009 Debacle exhibited a renewed interest in corporate take over actvities and re-purchase of the company's common stock to enhance the earnings per share potential.

With volatile securities markets, Johannes and the team recognized that the good old USA encouraged other countries to purchase Treasury securities so as to moderate the currency swings that impact export markets and the work place.

Some would say that these purchases of US Treasury securities by other countries were compelled by the US government to finance its out-of-control borrowing, in other words, a de facto tax for the rest of the world.

Alistair thought about this risk of unstable Japanese and German export revenues, and smiled frequently about this discussion with his cigarette-smoking group outside of his office located not far from the doomed WTC site – now a huge hole in the lower manhattan Wall Street area.

This Picture Doesn't Hang Straight

"Our crap on the heads of others stacked daily."

He added: "We really had good luck on this issue for years."

The smoking sessions lasted perhaps twenty to thirty minutes at a time. Johannes would learn much from these rather impromptu meetings – far more than the politically correct Drivel uttered in the formal Monday morning meetings.

The Board of Governors met often and included the management of the New York District to discuss future strategies ranging from wire transfer to examination policy.

This Committee would also review the facts and figures presented by its army of analysts, and the conclusions appeared in system wide communications.

Alistair held little respect for the statements of the Committee. The credibility of this group of men and women was almost zero.

Why, one could ask, because many of the research papers requested by the Washington DC Committee were pigeon holed in the desk drawers of the DC analysts.

The Oracle and his assistants wanted no Flack from its clientele regarding their controversial lending and trading activities. Besides, the Oracle and his internal lawyers had no appetite for legal challenges.

A certain direction for the course of the Nation was the real objective. For example, Johannes and the team were aware of the Goldman Sachs penchant for having many of its former employees become heads of various government agencies.

"Is it now clear to all of us the underlying reasoning for less supervision instead of more?"

Since the illiteracy of University graduates continues to increase, the Elitists derive from the "dumb and dumber" Youth the opportunity to change history, and customs and values long accepted by prior generations.

Johannes pondered over this development.

He fretted and thought about that phrase – the American Dream, but for whom, which group, and was the term twisted in meaning and used to manipulate the voting public?

Even crises are being created daily through the speeches of the usual suspects preaching a better world and provoking unrest to accomplish their own objectives. And they do it gladly!

The acumen of american financial management is emphasized as solid and to think otherwise would threaten the stability of the overall global system. One must take to heart the Gospel of the american way, their form of propaganda!

Today is another day, thought Johannes.

However, millions of investors continue to make the same mistakes – they drink from the same fountain fed by the piped water of the public media – and remain dependent on sales commission-oriented financial advisers.

On the other hand, in the 1950's during the polio epidemic, he remembered the debate on the dangers of too much sugar attacking the nervous system of young children, the powdered drink known as KoolAid was produced at low cost and provided a nice kick on very hot days.

Some countries would not import the drink.

Of course, the major media downplayed such negative reports as quackery! The beginning of fake news or dishonest reporting?

One newspaper in particular seemed to read like a national attempt to dumb down financial market discourse and real statistics on investor preferences.

Even the TV networks began to drink the Kool Aid, that is treat some circles of society as –out of touch.

Back to the subject of finance, thought Johannes.

Johannes looked at the almost always closed door opening to

Alistair O'Bannons office. Inside he utilized the sometimes speculative and confusing financial news items to his advantage.

Long known to him and Fernanda was the loss ridden portfolio of the largest mortgage banker – and the losses piled up against insufficient capital funds.

What else was new, thought the examination team.

They tried to report on the ever declining capital position of the Congress mandated mortgage support institutions - Federal National Mortgage Association and the Federal Home Loan Mortgage Corp.

Their management did not want to hear of such nonsense. They only dreamed of enormous political reward of making possible the American dream for everyone.

Such behavior proved to be detrimental to the credit quality of major lenders and to further loosen their credit standards for the benefit of greater increases in shareholder value. Also, the mortgages of the originating lender were quickly "tranched" into long term securities for the further distribution to the end investor.

In 1992 less financial backing was allowed by the regulators as default risk appeared minimal.

"I could absolutely vomit," he said, when he observed the free fall of stock values of Fannie and Freddie.

He had the same feeling on 9/11/2001, this time millions of people will suffer from the failure of these two institutions – the core of the American dream.

Johannes frowned and said: Again the regulator is the enemy of the public, it happens again and again!"

The investing community saw their opportunity quickly – short sales, always a superb vehicle to earn money on the backs of the lazy thinkers and malleable political hacks.

The short term gain potential improved dramatically when the SEC agreed with certain academicians and finance pros that it would not re-institute the up-tick rule to control short selling. Jubilant would be an understatement for Alistair and Fernanda's subsequent behavior after learning of this development.

To offset too much criticism for its action, the SEC reviewed other measures to control short term sales; this review lasted a year, and in the interim the financial markets in the wake of the 2008/2009 economic crisis realized losses in the Trillions of dollars.

None of the the measures found unanimous approval.

At home, Johannes, from the window of his "Study", observed a rather lean-looking squirrel feeding on acorns.

It was now spring of 2009. After a long winter, the woodpecker spent time on its perch, waiting to discover something interesting.

On the ground below, worms sought refuge from the hungry woodpecker.

Many other animals were also hungry: the fine people found nourishment from Caviar and Champagne.

Various social classes came together with a common objective: they must put something in their bellies.

For many of the middle class, the good paying jobs disappeared in favor of the low wage manufacturing and exporting countries.

The burgeoning demand to have something to eat compared unfavorably to the once attainable American dream,

The "security net" for those who cannot provide for themselves depended on substantial donations from the private sector; in 2008 a record 73 million pounds of foodstuffs were distributed to the homeless, aged and other needy persons.

These numbers increase annually as the average personal income declines.

While the media and the politicians focus on the solution to end hunger, the real issue is the continued job loss in the middle class.

Johannes mused at these clowns in the nation's capitol wringing their hands at the loss of middle class jobs, while the solutions are simple: stop the job loss to overseas cheap labor countries, start manufacturing domestically, enforce equilibrium or balanced trade globally – eliminate greedy trade balance surpluses and losses with trading partners.

He knew that the elite still wanted their pound of flesh, their appetites were insatiable, they gnawed steadily on that fatty piece, to rip off only the filet.

The total screwup in the American finance and regulatory structure impacted negatively certain countries in the EU, to mention a few examples.

The elitist community ripped off the filet, digested it fully, and left undigested scraps for the mass population.

In 2004 the negative Trend in the backwash of regulatory negligence could be seen in the so-called government "misery indices" of the EU: 13 percent of German citizens considered in the poverty zone, 11 million, of these children, the aged, those living alone were especially endangered, the former east Germany or the new provinces, so to speak, were significantly worse off than those in the old provinces – West Germany.

The middle class formed the lion's share of the misery indices, Austria, France and Belgium exhibited similar statistics.

Southern Europe showed more "misery" and Scandinavia appeared somewhat "better off", nevertheless this model of social happiness showed rising levels of poverty.

On this day, Alistair leafed through the thick credit file of Merck & Co. And found the article dated April 12, 2007, and discovered that the FDA decided not to approve the new drug, Arcoxia, the successor to Vioxx, due to new concerns over heart and circulation side effects.

However, a subsequent review by the Agency allowed the prescribing of the new drug on the basis of a last resort" if there were no alternatives to relatively safer" products!

THIS PICTURE DOESN'T HANG STRAIGHT

Two days before, Raffy brought the credit file to Alistair before any member of Johannes' team could review the file.

Alistair immediately bought 1,000 Shares before few traders were aware of the new assessment. In early trading, the share price climbed 1% to 46.20 USD.

Alistair became aware early on that Bayer AG, another leader in the field of pharmaceuticals, agricultural chemicals and other related products was well positioned to overcome the negatives of the current economic crisis.

He bought 1,000 shares. At the close of trading, it became the largest winner in the S&P 500 index!

He loved the alleged "toxic products!"

He also mused that it was "good to be me!"

He recognized that the country in this tense uncertain environment had succumbed to the wiles of the elitist speculators.

What was the value of honesty? Not much, he thought.

However, what really mattered to him was the value of insider information. For example, the issue of innoculations against the swine flu.

Alistair mused: the new ethic, which the media uses more and more, is to present a story which borders on the real truth of a situation.

In the field of Big Pharma, it is so useful to use this tactic, since few people pay attention to the daily "crap" published by Big Pharma, that the feared illness could spread globally, and the only solution was to initiate mass innoculations globally!

89

ADRIAN VOGT

However, recent preventive measures to counter this strain of flu responded positively to a centuries old remedy – the garlic bulb!

As evidence of the healing effect of the white bulb, which appeared in the local Serbian news media, large crowds at local music festivals confirmed only one case of the flu. The overwhelming majority of fans belonged to the younger generation, and large amounts of alcoholic beverages and marijuana were ingested.

Other large public gatherings confirmed no cases of the much dreaded flu strain. Also, the media mentioned the consumption of popular dishes laced liberally with garlic marinades and sauces.

This report of the serbian media and others in the EU did not please Alistair and Fernanda. Both knew the potential negative side effects of the Big Pharma solution to innoculate globally.

During this media coverage, other events caught their eye:

The Senate Committee process to appoint a new treasurer.

Alistair: this limp dick behaves like a fool, isn't that right?"

What is bothering him?"

Then he explained the non payment of federal income taxes of $34,000 during the years of 2001 - 2004!

He said: My mistakes were careless and avoidable. I was relying on the advice of my tax consultant. I should have been more pro-active."

Other issues included the hiring of a maid with questionable legal immigration status. In any case, he was appointed treasuer of the United States of America.

90

Alistair came to the conclusion that the Committee helped the limp dick out of a jam.

Alistair listened to Maria, one of the female commentators, as she spoke: "there is a huge deficit of ethical values, that I think the legislators tend toward acceptance, in order to just get along."

Alistair clicked the "off" button, leaned back in his leather chair, and stretched out his long arms.

Fernanda smiled and said: "we are finally getting rid of him."

Johannes observed daily the machinations of both, and became familiar with their "well, and?" attitude.

He muttered: "these shitheads, they exploit us all!"

When he became so "cranked up," over their external actions and inner attitude and their apparent bending of the truth, it began to impact his inner health; he must find consolation in something!

To bring this situation to light would be very difficult for him, he needed Wisdom and peace in his soul.

At this point, he allocated time to the **Holy Spirit**, he began to believe that the Crucifiction healed everyone over 2,000 years ago!

Yes! And Amen!

The books and scriptures in the Bible gave him courage to continue his work with evermore vigor! The many times sitting in the Iron Bird to Europe or Asia were no longer frustrating for him, he now had the Bible with him – the key to everlasting life!

He meditated on the fundamentals of Faith; FAITH will bring me to victory!

He decided to practice the perfect law of liberty in every aspect of his life: Believe the WORD of God – find out what he says about it. Say the WORD of God – Speak in agreement with Him when you talk about your situation. Act on the WORD of God – Take action based on what he says.

And, the final step: FORGIVE! Faith works best in a loving, forgiving Atmosphere.

Johannes would do his best to forgive the actions of the political and corporate elite, Alistair and Fernanda, and others; very difficult to do this, he thought.

Because they continue to steal from each and every one of us – the plundering of the Social Security fund, the excessive taxation, the career politician – the bane of this Republic!

He would forgive, but not forget!

Meetings with Alistair and Fernanda as well as their "ass kissing" buddies, sought agreement among the examination staff that the examinations be less "intrusive", in other words, carry out less work in the arena of control over new products and riskier trading activities as well as sub prime credit.

To control his anger over these developments, he considered leaving the room, and changing his dress shoes to running shoes. To reduce the level of cortisol and assist his immune system, he would jog at least two miles in the canyon of Wall Street.

He knew the common denominator of less stress: the realization of concrete results! Through this, he could list significant contributions to the team's performance, and recognize clearly the fruits of their work.

Nowadays he noticed fewer and fewer of his colleagues took sick days, apparently from fear of quietly being told that their services were no longer relevant to the new risk focused examination procedures.

After more than twenty years of service, they could no longer rely on the true intentions of their management.

Alistair and Fernanda conducted business via cell phone, these conversations could not be recorded. They behaved in an ice-cold manner, they wanted only their share.

These were difficult days and weeks, not the best of times, especially in the financial industry, actually in every branch of business.

For the global masses, the large enterprises spread doubt on life styles which might threaten their exploitative strategy.

These masters of the Universe had lost touch with the concept of money, they had forgotten what money was – bread, living space, a warm coat when it was cold, they lived via credit and debit cards.

For example, forty percent of the enterprises in the US plan no wage increases, although workers in India and Asia have more money in their pockets.

One must be competitive and free market oriented, so the Executives began to favor shipping American jobs overseas.

Of course, not mentioned was the required adjustment assistance provided by the government for displaced workers whose jobs were shifted overseas.

Oh, yes, The executives simply ignored these re-training rules; the politicians were bought and paid for!

Details, details. These are global solutions to the increases in shareholder value, opined the Smart Money."

This band of elitist pols and businessmen and women are the real terrorists, thought Johannes and his team.

Behind closed doors they can fashion their strategy of market expansion and contraction, distribution of work skills, capital and technology. And even the decision to purchase their own shares to enhance earnings per share was discussed.

Their park avenue meeting place is home to many of these insiders and executives. And, for protection from prying eyes and ears, other buildings in Manhattan became home to some of these decison makers – named after american colleges of the Ivy League realm.

Alistair listened carefully to the analyses since sometimes he had to rely on intuition rather than "cold hard facts" prior to purchasing shares.

He was a true speculator in the sense of not being swayed by the latest research and technical analyses. He was a true contrarion.

He did not like the printed investor services, Hell, the printer knew more than the reading public!

The various TV business channels provided some insight to "hot ideas."

He considered the case of Citibank. Within the FRBNY, he sought out the Central Point of Contact (CPC), a rather portly woman who was promoted internally way too fast, for her stock of knowledge, but that was one of the "Rules of the Road" – to improve diversity and provide equal opportunity to move up the promotion ladder.

He considered her predictions as worthy of belief; however, much of the content of her voluminous pages of statistics and opinions of account officers, appeared to correspond more to the new examination guidelines, which he considered to be page filler and the conclusions seemed more "Glitter than Substance."

He immediately conducted a short sale of several thousand shares! In short, her reporting provided the impetus to satisfy his hunger for a quick profit. The more he traded, the better he felt – it seemed to raise his testosterone level.

However, some psychologists described his compulsive behavior as a character weakness. He would think otherwise.

On that morning in March, he felt that familiar RUSH.

He read about the still in the news, alleged swine flu epidemic.

This report is way too long, he muttered.

He read the first two parapgraphs and the last two paragraphs to glean the gist of the epidemic.

"The inhabitants of La Gloria, Veracruz, Mexico, were impacted severely, and responsible for the outbreak. A large pig farm came under focus, although the Mexican authorities did not confirm the source."

Reason: for several years, the populace of La Gloria complained of the terrible stench from the 5 mile removed pig farm, whose 18 giant stalls contained over 15, 000 pigs."

According to other media outlets, people were afraid of contamination of the air and water, however, the main owner of the farm, Smithfield Foods, downplayed the situation since the

ADRIAN VOGT

local people were uneducated and not capable of making correct judgments!

Alistair finished reading the April 2009 report, and learning of more flu cases in Mexico, bought the shares of Gilead Sciences, GlaxoSmithKline and Novavax.

At that time, Johannes pursued the News about a possible Pandemic, and he wondered why other toxic substances in the air were not researched?

Big Pharma-supported scientists would opine that these did not have the testing to determine, if in combination with other viruses, a valid threat to the environment existed.

Johannes also inquired of the scientists conducting the tests, and with whom they would be working to find real solutions.

The media did not even consider such a possibility.

Then on April 27, 2009, another report indicated more swine flu cases, and these raised fears of a flu epidemic, and investment markets recorded hefty paper losses, as tourism and air travel was predicted to plummet.

At first glance, investors remembered the negative results of the much publicized lung disease – Severe Acute Respiratory Syndrome (SARS), discovered in Asia in 2003, which led to a global crisis.

Volatility became the trading opportunity for many, and simultaneously, the share price of the largest bank in Germany soared to new heights as a 25 percent return on equity before tax seemed a reality for the long term!

Well, maybe, thought Johannes.

96

As it turned out the middle class was still shrinking. And these remaining workers were severely impacted as the equity in their homes began to melt like butter in the hot sun!

The Fiasco in real estate was fueled by the everlasting belief that home prices never declined for the simple reason: risk was well distributed throughout the country, no one would give up the American dream.

Of course, from the very beginning, this argument was flawed, and turned out to be a Myth!

Perhaps the greatest Swindle of all time was the absence of a complete review of real estate portfolios, the supporting documents, and the marketability of the underlying collateral.

The oracle previously opined on the soundness of the above theory. After all, he argued, regulation could not stop any developing crisis, it was incumbent on the lenders to do their due diligence, and immediately address operations problems internally.

Well, OK, if one follows that line of thought.

And Johannes and his team tested vigorously the operational integrity and discovered weaknesses pointing to gross negligence of the lenders.

Their examination reports and detailed asset quality reviews spelled TROUBLE for the examined banks.

The oracle contacted some of the major banks that packaged these substandard assets, the closed door sessions with bank management had the effect of never reporting the true nature of the still brewing crisis.

Their reports never got past Alistair and Fernanda.

Not surprising, since financial terrorism is alive and well.

Johannes left the rather imposing building located accross the street from the Fortress, affectionately known for its well guarded presence in the Wall Street district.

The streets at half past seven in the evening were still busy with fashionably dressed men and women, most people would pass them in the street and not realize what these men and women were capable of, thought Johannes.

But he knew them, the new face of Evil, some would even say: Satan's minions.

The Wall Street Yuppies and the blowhards of Washington DC are joined together in an unholy alliance for their own self centered agenda – one to have their fair share of wealth, and the other to be re-elected.

Their Motto: what's yours is mine.

Walking through the throng of the crowd to reach the way home, he mused that it should not surprise anyone that a crisis becomes a starting point for these Elitists.

Finally home with his beautiful Alischraga, he discussed with her the developing real estate and health crises.

The physical and financial health globally is being impacted by our own habits and living conditions," said Johannes.

The wall Street Journal headlined both threats to the status quo: the dangerous dust from dried out fecal matter on the streets of Mexico City, mixed with the tiny particles of industrial and automobile activity, human sweat and flatulence, which together brewed a cocktail of toxic substances, permeated the air and water!

The report of April 28, 2009 revealed that air pollution in several large cities, despite the "Green Revolution" had reached unhealthy levels.

According to the report, 6 of 10 Americans must visit regularly hospitals for treatment for persistent coughing, heart failure, lung cancer, and early death.

Alistair and Fernanda also read the same article, and recognized the potential of huge short term gain in Big Pharma.

Statistics are sometimes exaggerated to garner the public attention, especially the treatment costs of Cancer – from $1.3 billion in1963 to $72 billion!

Aids, malaria, influenza, and a polluting environment would provide more and more opportunities for obtaining their fair share of the wealth.

Alistair knew that control of information meant power. And the war for the control of man's ideals and ideas raged further.

He found the situation very unsettling.

Although he was not totally without scruples, he thought often of a more toxic global environment and knew the increased danger to the general Health of the world via a global industrialized society.

Alistair acknowledged that few of the so-called experts discuss publicly the daily consumption of heavy metals, chemicals, drugs, artificial preservatives and overly processed foods, etc. which tend to burden the human body.

Alistair mused: toxic junk in the colon, toxic credit losses! It makes sense!

The mix of good and bad credit ratings of the collateral in the mortgage backed securities market, resembles closely the mix of foul smelling human fecal matter and other gaseous materials, converting to dust particles that overpower the local sweet smelling perfume of tropical plants.

"The balance of good and evil is really distorted, it remains temporarily disquieting so that WE can cash in on the upcoming opportunies, "said Alistair.

His feeling was correct. He grinned broadly - fanfare AND uncertainty, an almost perfect storm for quick speculative gain!

The paper for Merck and Qiagen climbed quickly on the basis of a vaccine and a new antibiotic to counteract the swine flu.

Similarly, the usual bought and paid for actors could also profit handsomely from the expected bailout of the sloppy operations of the major banks. They were the insiders!

However, they read another opinion which stated that other reasons might be responsible for the outbreak.

They were not pleased to find out that a prominent immunologist and expert in matters of animal diseases and control disagreed on the cause of the swine flu.

They read his thesis for the sicknesses and learned quickly that the speculative fervor could have a short life!

The well known Director of Public Health and Animal Protection Society opined:

"The only time that a swine flu virus of this type occurred was in 1998 at a massive pig farm, where the swine, human and bird viruses were seen as a potential connection."

The Doctor noted that the size of the farm compared to a football field, there were 5,000 female pigs forced into metal boxes and stalls – they could not move around freely, nose against nose, laying in their own excrement, so to speak, a potential breeding ground for serious diseases.

He stated: "it is certainly reasonable to assume that something similar occurred in Mexico."

"Furthermore, the Threat to the health of the general population of these huge pig farms is made possible via the size of these operations which enhance greatly the transfer of viruses."

He explained that the stress to the animal immune system due to the filthy conditions of the pig farm could be alleviated with simple cost effective measures: the laying of straw on the cold cement floor to relieve the laming effect of the cold cement floor.

The reduction of contamination to other animals proved considerable!

The Doctor noted also that overcrowding, insufficient sunlight and fresh air increased the traumatic conditions of the animals which contributed to the spreading of this contagion among the human population.

All of these factors combined, warned the Doctor, could imitate the model of the 1918 Pandemic, and might result in the creation of other animal viruses of a more serious nature, as millions of animals – chickens, turkeys, cows, etc. are being held in these massive holding pens, forced fed, administered antibiotics under disgusting conditons until their slaughter.

Several scientific associations and the United Nations issued press reports in 2005 against these massive industrial livestock

ADRIAN VOGT

breeding and retention operations. The substance of these reports centered on the potential development of dangerous viral forms over time.

In 2008, the Pew Commission on Industrial Farm Animal Production, in which the former Agriculture Commisioner participated, disclosed unacceptable risks to the general health of the Population through the practice of the fattening of animals prior to slaughter.

These surroundings promote the virus in the case of chickens and pigs, and if little is done to prevent these conditions, then a 1918 type of pandemic might occur.

The Study concluded that if we are serious about protecting human health, then the closing of these types of factory operations could prevent a type of pandemic similar to the Spanish flu pandemic of 1918, the deadliest in history, which infected an estimated 500 million people worldwide—about one-third of the planet's population—and killed an estimated 20 million to 50 million victims, including some 675,000 Americans.

Aside from the threat of sickness, the mass feeding operations are perceived as inhumane where billions of our animal friends are atrociously slaughtered.

Of course, Alistair did not like this study, and feared it might delay his first IPO. Also, the doctor conducting these studies was a vegetarian!

But he did not worry about potential legislation aimed at factory farms and the mass animal breeding and feeding operations, since he could rely on certain Washington DC politicians to block any such laws.

102

"Now we can be ready to really rock and roll," declared Alistair.

The Impulse to launch this IPO came quickly. However, the consumer protection people voiced opposition to the appointment of the Under Secretary of Food Safety at the Department of Agriculture.

Their Reasoning: the candidate for this position is a long time supporter of food irradiation.

Alistair yelled: "Fuck off, Asshole!"

Alistair often talked to himself when he had to react on a decision that might impact his pocketbook.

He enjoyed his Status as one of the participants, who really understood the Washington politicians and their Wall Street benefactors, he could sniff out the newest conspiracy and the tendency to fraud. He recognized the new penchant for behind the scenes intrigue as the next Swindle.

"He should keep his mouth shut," said Alistair to Fernanda as they watched the Vice President of the United States opine on his version of the causes of swine flu.

"He's such a fucking fool to make these statements!"

"I would tell my family to stay away from Mexico, stay away from confining areas, stand in open areas, when coughing or sneezing, never congregate in small areas, etc."

The Vice President hit the nail on the head! Of course, the fickle Media criticized him for telling the truth.

The Vice President rambled on: "limited space, roominess at a premium, and no green space for the animals. It is Torture for the animals."

He blathered on as if he was up for re-election. He is the same person that accused the opposite side of the aisle as southern landowners leaving their slaves in chains!

Perhaps he will garner a moral profit?

Or, he will join the forces of Greed and be a purveyor of financial terrorism.

He could also state that the Swine Flu is an illusion and the regulators have the situation under control.

The regulators must do something to re-build its reputation, mused the Vice President.

He hoped that few people would recall the tragic events of October 2008, when the Congress and their regulators could have avoided the Subprime Crisis via careful and detailed reviews of mortgage asset portfolios, as required in prior years.

Good people who played by the rules and lived within their means lost most of their equity in their homes, and hopes for a decent retirement.

"Certainly over the years, they really screwed the pooch," said Alistair. The Savings and Loan Crisis and the almost failure of the hedge fund Long Term Capital Management (LTCM) were clearly on the minds of investors.

Big Difference, tho, stated Johannes, who assisted the clean up process in both cases.

LTCB was rescued with hefty contributions from the Capital-owners!

Subprime credits collateralized with dicey equity approved by so-called <u>Robo</u> signers at the lending instutuion were bailed out by the taxpayer!

"To wipe the egg off their faces, perhaps the regulators would concoct a new crisis, act on it, in order to rescue its reputation from disrepute," said the pretty Media commentator, who jubilantly declared on July 7, 2010: "the best week for share prices in this sector since July 2008!"

Hardly good news for the home owner, whose loan to value ratio in most cases exceeded 100 percent!

Johannes recalled also the **alternative** plan to rescue the lenders: use the taxpayer money to payoff all substandard mortgages, including the under water" credits, in this way the home owner could be made whole" and the lenders wipe the bad loans off their balance sheets.

Nice, if it happened, thought Johannes.

Johannes used his forefinger to separate the first page from the rest of the voluminous credit file to read about the significant buildup of vaccine inventories produced by this large participant in the "Big Pharma" segment of the U.S economy.

However, he learned of the risks associated with the swine flu epidemic, if it existed at all.

Within the first months of 2010, this question remained in the minds of many.

Division of opinion of the severity of this virus still remained.

105

The WHO maintained that one-third of the world's population could be susceptible.

However, by May 2010 many of the impacted countries already had the wave of swine flu cases behind them; therefore, little demand existed for expensive vaccinations, and some of these countries government budgets could not afford the cost.

And there was no effort to provide these Vaccine supplies at little cost. One article in the file strengthened the belief that scientists with Big Pharma had pressured the WHO to issue pandemic warnings!

Unfortunately the WHO actions led to several countries spending vast sums of money on insufficiently tested vaccines.

The much heralded coming Pandemic provided Big Pharma a Jackpot" for potential earnings windfall.

The Article also pointed out the Pushback" of some experts who claimed the WHO changed its Criteria for designating a Pandemic: not so much the danger of the Virus, but the speed of the Outbreak."

Johannes looked up and spoke to the team in this manner: "Am I dreaming?"

"Are we witnessing the intentions of men with evil intent who want to speculate at the expense of the health of the global population?"

"Profit over the people's general Health and well being?"

"Is it the Instrument of this Madness?

"Open Borders policy in place, despite the possibility of the Virus spreading quickly, knowing no boundary?"

His heart began to beat rapidly!

"The experts predicted a recovery in the securities markets," so the same pretty commentator.

"But who are the experts," questioned Bill.

On the evening of 14 July, 2009, Bastille Day in France, the clever boys and girls with the FRBNY – the new Yuppies, many wearing the fashionable medium sized round lensed eye glasses, manipulated the numbers of the balance sheet of the FRB to indicate trading profits.

Wait a minute, said Bill. But, for whom?

Bank holding companies that were investment firms prior to the crisis, now came under the alleged supervision of the FRBNY.

They spread the Myth of being too big to fail.

They walked into the Fortress and utilized the Discount Window, submitting collateral, much of it mortgage backed securities, and borrowed Billions of Dollars at very low rates.

"The Public be damned", yelled Bill.

Bill rolled up the sleeves of his tailor made dress shirt, and one could see his enormous biceps.

Summertime in Manhattan caused one on occasion to do this, especially when the temperature reached 100 degrees Fahrenheit.

Sometimes the air conditioning systems of the older buildings on Park Avenue relied on vents that were too long and the system worked harder to transport the cooler air.

Johannes thought initially that Bill was going to punch someone out.

Good candidates for a thorough thrashing were these smart ass yuppies. Some bragged openly that their relatives had survived the Depression years and built up their fortunes via clever trading schemes.

O.K. Fair enough, the team thought. We all want to earn a profit, but fairly.

However, the team began to question the statements of some of these Yuppies, one, in particular: "We have large plans for all people!"

They also bragged about their inclusive nature, political correctness, and willingness to strictly abide by the FRBNY "Rules of the Road."

The Yuppies' Army of analysts celebrated the news of one very large investment firm that it earned a Billion Dollars during the Subprime crisis, calling correctly the failure of the regulators to police their banks properly- they simply sold short their investments in mortgage backed securities.

Not against the law, these firms regulated by the SEC could trade long or short for their clients.

Silently the politicians on both sides of the aisle also followed suit.

With this news, Alistair and Fernanda squared their positions and cashed out.

The team knew which group was thrown out of the boat to swim with the sharks.

Alistair und Fernanda knew the consequences of such a policy, in the style of the former chairman of Citibank: the most powerful sharks would swallow the smaller fish whole.

The next evening- July 15, 2009, the Champagne bubbled, and the diamonds worn by the fine guests glittered prominently.

At this Gala, the former First Lady and her Husband, the President of the United States lectured the guests:

"In Reality, America is not a mature marketplace. It is dependent on its ability to be able to borrow money, although like any spoiled child, it has not earned the right to do so."

"One day, the party will end, and this child will no longer get the easy money."

"Gold and Silver sparkles in the Sun, even like a romantic candlelight dinner!"

"Pontificating Bastards," whispered Alistair to his beautiful Brazilian spouse, Rosa. Fernanda also smiled, and agreed with them that the tax payer-funded former First Family should at least praise the voluntary fund raising efforts of this Charity.

Alistair, Rosa und Fernanda smiled like Cheshire Cats as they met and greeted their friends and others at this Benefit Gala, which the Sponsor stated that the proceeds would be for a "good purpose."

They listened respectfully as she spoke:

"From our viewpoint we see a "beautiful new World" as more and more people allow themselves to be inoculated with the newest

Vaccines being tested globally against various conditions including overweight, tooth decay, sneezing, coughing, inflammation, diarrhea, etc.."

"Over 600 new vaccines may be available to the public, the production of these miracle substances is similar to a large, red Bud on a rose bush to its complete bloom," as she gushed with excitement.

The guests noticed saliva on the corners of her mouth, as she continued her speech, a slight drool began. Some of the crowd took handkerchiefs and wiped the corners of their mouths to gain her attention. She noticed! And she adroitly wiped the corners of her large mouth in response.

At the conclusion of her Appeal for donations to this very worthy cause, the audience clapped enthusiastically.

Of particular interest to the threesome, was the comment: "if side effects develop and persist, the treatment of such could signify further financial support for the continued humanitarian efforts of the Pharmaceutical industry."

At the conclusion of this Event, the last of the guests hesitated at the door, before their leaving, and to the Pair the threesome stated: "you both have a good heart to donate so much of your time and money."

"Thank you," they beamed with gratitude for these remarks, as they left the large auditorium.

For the global poor, they had received donations in excess of $500,000.

The O'Bannon Family belonged to the Group of

"One-Percenters", who possessed an unfair advantage over 99 percent of the population.

Members of this Group usually graduated from the London School of Economics.

As one of these, Alistair usually benefitted from "interesting investment opportunities."

The "One-Percenters" were able to afford the Best of the best Investment Advisers, dine in the finest restaurants, own vacation houses in the Tropics, and drive the fastest cars.

And the 99 percent got their information from uninformed friends and family members as well as the established media and publishing outlets, the latter proving to be incorrect most of the time.

Many of Alistair's information sources did not recommend investing long term, only short term trading, since the domestic outlook currently was not favorable for the long term investor.

They noticed that Lululemon Athletic became one of the Wall Street Darlings, as the firm reported tripled earnings per share for the latest quarter, and beat the Street's best estimates!

Because of the continued good ratios and prospects they held their positions and added to them.

Alistair and Fernanda felt comfortable that few analysts dared to mention other positive factors: cost savings via offshoring of jobs and cancelled pension benefits which contributed to sizeable increases in per share profit.

Such information never appeared in shareholder reports, thank goodness, thought Alistair.

ADRIAN VOGT

If one begins to ask the question: how would one think or behave, if one works in a management environment that focuses only on profit at any cost.

Johannes and his team were still reviewing corporate credit files and financial statements at the Institution's mid-town location, when Alistair returned to his 23rd floor office down town.

He whispered something as he sat down in the leather upholstered chair by the window and stared for a few minutes at the giant dark hole in the ground, in which the WTC at one time stood majestically as its towers sometimes pierced the morning fog and low hanging clouds.

His corner office adjoined a large conference room and served as a discussion forum for all his operations staff and personnel assigned to examine certain domestic and foreign banks and securities firms.

The more than three hours meeting had really achieved nothing. He was pissed that Fernanda kept interrupting to bring forward HER ideas about risk focused eaminations.

She said: "Supporting workpapers and documents should be carefully formulated and arranged to provide the Basis for the Content of the Examination."

Fernanda and her ass-kissing examination staff occupied themselves daily with writing style and content, in which the analyst and examiner should recommend no prescriptive action which would require extensive followup.

"Verbs like "must and should" that characterize the urgent and serious nature of corrective measures, are "Taboo", she said.

She insisted that every examination report for the bank's

112

management must add value to the bank's operation, and the Report should not contain operational deficiencies or weaknesses disclosed by the examiners that could be construed as an attitude of "Gotcha!"

Again, she made it clear to the staff that contested weaknesses could be mild in nature, and certain critical comments should be "watered down" to show the supervised institution that the regulators are compassionate with their clients!

Fernanda represented the NEW UNDERSTANDING that the banks and other supervised entities operate in highly competitive situations that allow a relaxed policy of supervision. Followup reviews of management's corrective actions would also be minimized.

Johannes and his team had already adjusted to the new guidelines. They unanimously agreed that the relaxed approach for the client entities could well bite her in the ass. Of course, she would try to postpone any negative results of this perceived negligence.

Alistair lit his Bio-Cigarette, puffed several times to enjoy the taste of the rich tobacco. The smoke wafted gently up into the ventilation ducts from his office to other sections of the 23rd floor.

Nobody complained, since there were more pressing issues on which one must focus.

More puffs, as he watched the current news on his computer. The commentator said: "The USA lost six million jobs to overseas locations, the country is indebted by more than $1.4 Trillion, and the imports of cheap consumer goods rose again, of which, so the opinion of the commentator, belong in the trash containers!"

The Deacon of the Cox Busineess School of Southern Methodist University commented that the continued loss of household wealth, reduced access to credit, would depress consumption further.

Alistair reasoned that more chaos, unemployment, and little change in the congressional and senate balance of power would make **more opportunities for short term trading.**

The country was still embroiled in Iraq and Afghanistan, factions fighting over health Care, declining home prices, rising food and energy costs, tighter credit conditions, turbulent share prices, and Helicopter Ben and his female sidekick continued their deflationary Blather.

He also came to the conclusion that the current political Elite provided for a measure of "timeless corruption."

For Rosa and Alistair everything went according to plan, they had made the correct financial decisions.

Nevertheless, they would not buy those expensive yoga mats from Lululemon!

Timeless Corruption

When Johannes thinks of dishonest behavior his heart begins to burn around the edges!

For solace and support for his daily activities, his thoughts turn to the greatest book ever written – the Bible.

Today, he turned to Chapter 17 in the Book of Revelations which discusses the perverse ways of important people that have succumbed to the Entities of Evil.

Johannes was determined to be victorious over the wayward ways of his management. As a Soldier in the Army of the Lord he would not quit – this was not an Option.

He then turned to Psalm 101 to gain courage in his fight to overcome those deceitful individuals seeking to destroy the original purpose of the central bank's supervision efforts.

He also remembered the advice of the Spanish Philosopher, Jose Ortega y Gasset, author of the Revolt of the Masses, who said:

"Life is a series of collisions with the future; it is not the sum of what we have been, but what we yearn to be."

"The type of human being we prefer reveals the contours of our heart."

Like the Sun, which always rises in the East, and appears on the Horizon, the stately Central Bank is always there for its Citizenry, or so it would appear.

It stands for everything monetary and endeavors to fulfill its purpose, as delegated by the American congress: full employment, price stability and prosperity.

It is there for all to see. The heavy doors at the main entrance stand in harmony with the powerful people who occupy the 10th floor of this fortress-like building.

The management enjoyed its own self-made Hubris from its in 1998 managed rescue of the LTCM hedge fund, which gross mismanagement by the so-called hedge fund experts almost caused a financial crisis.

However the dark clouds appear over the Horizon again as this sector ten years later still has not found the courage to implement optimal operating controls to safeguard assets.

As several large hedge funds are now owned by some of the most prestigious banks in the world, Johannes and his team must now - once again - disclose the not too risk averse environment in this sector. They would not quit.

The deficiency in documentary support remains, and the approval of new business still outstrips the operational ability to monitor it.

Thanks to the "Mercy" of the Federal Reserve Bank of New York, this problem remains unresolved.

Unexpected trading losses of counterparties that contracted with the hedge fund could spell disaster, particularly if supporting contract documents cannot be located!

This Picture Doesn't Hang Straight

Such a thought made top management of the FRBNY quite nervous, but not agitated enough to introduce "real" supervisory constraints on future new business.

The Financial times of May 3, 2007 echoed the most recent warning about the insufficiency of documents.

Since 2002, the hedge fund industry exhibited investment asset value of $1.5 Trillion!

Johannes and his team continued to bring this problem to the attention of hedge fund management, whose reply always seemed to be that we have a good idea of our potential counterparty exposure.

Hello! You don't know for certain who the contract was sold to or bought from?!

The several serious deficiencies presented to FRBNY management did not result in supervisory action other than a "frank" discussion with hedge fund management.

But not to fear, the Oracle, after 18 years as Chairman of the FRB Governors will now function as an advisor with Paulson & Co., a NYC hedge fund that exhibited in 2007 substantial profit for its investors, a result of taking the opposite position against sub-prime mortgage backed securities.

Nevertheless, some Advisors expressed disdain over the continued lack of operations skills and relevant technology that still could not confirm same day trading volumes until two to three days later.

The Street began to question why the FRBNY still allowed this unsatisfactory condition to persist.

A good question, thought Johannes. Could it be that there is

ADRIAN VOGT

more Glitter than Substance with the enforcement capabilities of its top management?

Outside, Johannes noted the brewing rain storm, the wind became stronger, larger raindrops fell, and hail stones pounded the windows.

Behind the scenes decision-making seemed to be the rule of the day, and there was no one to act as a note taker in these meetings!

How in "H" do you know what transpired in these discussions?

The sky did not begin to clear. The rain endured all night. Lightning defined the dark clouds overhanging the City.

The brightness of early morning was a welcome sight. And the high water mark remained intact.

To this day, the transparency of hedge funds operations remained opaque. All efforts to supervise this industry had failed. The White House and the Congress announced in unison: "we do not need more laws."

The new Oracle, Helicopter Ben expressed on April 12, 2007, the same nonsense: "preferable to new oversight, is the current system for hedge funds."

"Helicopter?"

The team: "Watching from above?

"A superficial View of the financial markets?"

"Reliance on external sources, other regulators, and external auditors to perform the examination work?"

The Umbrella Inspector of all entities operating in the financial field, as described by the Oracle: "is revolutionary. It brings a diversified and refreshing view of banking supervision!"

The Oracle was known for his daily dips in his old fashioned bath tub – something similar to those in the Cialis ads. An avid tennis player, playing for hours at a time, his back needed the rest in epsom salts water.

The oracle was comfortable with the GLB, since it promoted cooperation with other supervisory agencies, the days of arguing over the financial strength ratings to be assigned to the institution were over!

Now the investment bankers and their banks – vice a versa – can feel free to reap as much profit as possible, the regulators were now sympathetic to their competive nature in the global market place.

"These pussies now could argue about the cost of doing business, never mind the operational accuracy of processing transactions," said Bill.

Some years later, Johannes remembered those painful days of accepting a much looser policy of supervision.

He reminded the team of their purpose as the Remnant Faithful: "We renounce irreligion and worldly passions. We are zealots for good deeds."

The new Oracle – Helicopter Ben, enjoyed fiddling with the lower part of his "salt and pepper" beard during discussions of risk before an audience of economists and visiting supervisors from various countries.

In support of his argument that the large Hedge Funds need

no expanded regulation because investors through GLB have discovered better ways to manage risks - they have become more mature technically and are in a better position to handle challenging situations.

Yeah. Sure, thought the team.

This new philosophy could have prevented the Subprime Crisis and the embarrassing failure of the "me too" Rating Agencies – S&P, Moody's, Fitch, as well as the Crash in the financial markets!

The team asked themselves: "is he – Bernanke, the successor to the old Oracle - Greenspan, an Idiot or is he for real?"

Johannes prayed that what he said would be proven true. The Theory of the economic man always being correct in his/her behavior was tested.

The team endeavored to have the new Oracle visit the examination site to gain the proper view of the supervised entity's true financial condition. It never came to pass!

The predecessor never visited any examination site, preferring instead to rely on the judgement of the numerous analysts that filled the several floors of the Washington DC edifice.

Also, he relied primarily on the reports of the examined entities, since it was incumbent on the entity's senior management to file accurate information.

The independent external auditors were in the best position to validate the "numbers"; however these – net worth, assets and liabilities, income and expense, etc. were confirmed only at year end, and frequently not punctually presented to the institution's management.

What we are really hearing, thought Johannes, is that unaudited information is the basis for earnings per share, shareholder value, and share price estimates!

One of the first pronouncements by the Oracle's Successor occurred in Independence Hall, Philadelphia, Pennsylvania, sometimes referred to as the City of Brotherly Love.

With every word, that flowed out of his rounded mouth, which was encircled with a well manicured "salt and pepper" beard, he would emphasize to his audience, that the careful scrutiny on the part of investors was preferable to new regulations!

Hard to believe that the new Central Bank Chairman would support this idea.

Perhaps he was thinking of the "dead certain" ratings of listed and unlisted securities by the Ratings Agencies, which advice was contained in its research reports subscribed by the major financial institutions.

What was wrong with that SITUATION?

Was it a gross CONFLICT OF INTEREST?

Or could one also view this arrangement as incestuous?

Or the evil behavior on the part of all participants in the Financial industry?

Johannes thought that one might overlook the negatives if one was allowed to scold publicly the transgressing banks and their subsidiaries, for example.

The worst Sin of all, which the team reasoned was the new

policy of looking the other way, intentional overlooking of facts, and non adherence to supervisory regulations year after year!

In other words, operational weaknesses indentified by the examination team and the internal audit staff could remain unresolved for years!

Supervised entity management could, **behind closed doors,** arrange with FRBNY management the decision not to follow the team's recommendations since the issues were – somehow already known, and entity management was already making strides to correct these challenging operational issues, and, therefore, these identified weaknesses were challenges for the entire industry!

In more than one case, Johannes recalled objections to his team's findings with this response:

"If the team came down too hard on us on these weaknesses, it would appear that we were the whipping boy of the FRBNY!"

Also: "After all, our staff doesn't have the time to file reports to keep the FRBNY fully apprised of any problem considered serious as required in the supervisory manuals!"

Johannes: "Or are problems intentionally overlooked so that no "difficult" issue comes to the surface?

While the new Oracle pontificated further, Johannes thought more and more of the now endless Zeal of his male and female bosses at the FRBNY to completely restructure the Bank Supervision Department.

Of course, this experiment with a supervisory model as discussed earlier with the management staff by that Columbia University Professor, that has served the industry well for years, would fail.

He likened this thought with the not too infrequent stray gun shots one heard in the neighboring cities of Philadelphia and Camden.

Most of the time **they had no direction**, piercing the walls of empty industrial buildings and war zone like structures.

Yes, indeed. Philadelphia, the City of Brotherly Love, the City of many possibilities, at least the Chamber of Commerce, thought so.

Hello, Hello ?!!

Almost daily the noise of automatic weapons interrupted the still of morning.

For a time, student truancy reached a crisis point, as large numbers of inner city students rampaged in the shopping malls, beating up shoppers and tourists with their fists, school girls in their skirts kicking and spitting on the fallen, and cursing loudly.

These images did not play well for a city allegedly known for its brotherly love, and the proponents of this misleading propaganda, scurried around like rats running from flood waters, to offer solutions: "the suburban elite should have their children attend the high schools of the inner city to fully complement their education!"

This talk sounded strangely familiar.

Both Oracles heralded the concept of diversified risks in a portfolio of investments, to enhance the comfort level of investors.

Johannes: "Cool, perhaps the city fathers and the responsible law enforcement officials could perform their duties and place these troublemakers back in school, and encourage the study of useful ideas."

"Yes, if the responsible regulators of the financial industry are allowed to carry out their work."

He became restless in his chair listening to the end of the new Oracle's speech to the Group, which seemed to echo the **new supervisory model.**

He sighed loudly. The team knew that the days of unannounced surprise visits were long gone – the Principle of Cause and Effect were no more!"

On May 15, 2008, Helicopter Ben spoke before a conference of bankers in Chicago on the necessity of improved Risk Management systems.

He droned: "institutions granting credit need to strengthen their ability to discover risks, especially those related to subprime loans."

Also in attendance was the team, who discussed silently among themselves that the speech was the same old line espoused in the several large volumes of FRB manuals discussing risk.

And these manuals were already available to all interested parties via various internet websites!

Hello! Hello! Is anyone home?

At intermission, the team quietly left the large auditorium to meet with their immediate Boss, Alistair O'Bannon.

Apparently, they were all on the "same wave length" as Alistair grinned broadly, flailing his hands in the air and saying: "this Prick is saying nothing!"

"The new Caesar of the Central Bank is stating the obvious!"

"Ya gotta get paid back, you dumb fuck!"

"That's the end result of all lending!"

"The ultimate basis of a lender's Shareholder Value!"

"Are the lenders performing proper due diligence to determine the ability of the borrower to repay?"

The team listened respectfully, as Alistair raged on about the basics of risk taking and reporting, and adequate reserves and capital to protect against potential losses.

Several thoughts came to mind as they listened further.

Alistair is like a Chameleon – a change in circumstance, and behavior came to mind.

They knew of his penchant for short term trading, taking advantage of known weaknesses of the traded target, and the deep knowledge of an "insider."

Alistair continued: "The subprime borrower was typically egged on by the lender – realize the "American Dream", it was OK to spend more than you earn, as excessive consumption drove the Gross National Product (GNP) to ever larger growth rates."

The team began to turn over in its collective Psyche with certain Revelations:

"Always leading to economic crises, were false promises and overspending."

"The parallels to the present real estate crisis were uncontested."

"The American sickness of over-consumption and little saving leads to social unrest, and in extreme cases, the severe decline in a nation's will to survive."

"Without discipline no individual and a country can determine its own destiny."

The team now knew that their government – in fact, any government is the enemy. It lacks basic integrity. It commits daily to financial terrorism against its citizens!

The alleged Protector of the whole economy has fallen prey to the Temptation of ignoring problems that are real in the minds of the borrower – in particular, the stupid ones undertaking debt from loosely regulated lenders to whom prompt repayment would prove to be an illusory event.

More Glitter than substance became the team's conclusion about its own government!

As the Exhortations of Helicopter Ben began to end, the team noticed that the weather outside changed radically: low hanging dark clouds, then light rain, dreary, then sunny once again!

The origin of the cyclical nature of weather, calm and stormy, was respected by no one, at least not publicly.

As Johannes listened patiently to Alistair, he mulled over and over again, the purpose of the GLB and the alleged enforcement of its provisions. The new regulatory environment was becoming ever more permissive for the actions of the regulated entity. Political correctness seemed to dominate the new policy and enforcement.

O.K. How is the new trend to be stopped? His thinking was interrupted by Alistair stating: I'm done with this Shit!"

Finally, thank goodness, Alistair is done talking.

Today's date, the 25th of June 2007, was no special day, except more reporting on the common Misery experienced by certain groups in our society and the unforeseen consequences of such is becoming more prevalent.

That evening the message from his subconscious disturbed him greatly. The periodic dreams gave him anxiety and stress.

At the same time, it forced him to think of the future.

The nightmares could be the result of a real life trauma, the sequence of events is still affecting me, thought Johannes. Does it signify a warning of negative events? Does it mean some colleagues do not wish me well?

That evening Johannes dreamed about animals, huge creatures, which showed their teeth in a threatening way.

The leader of the Group, a Dobermann, a majestic-looking dog came close to me, and said:

Johannes, we have great plans, breathtaking plans, which will bring you Ecstasy! Come, howl with us!"

Suddenly, he cowered before me and went into a squat position, his muscular back legs quivered, and on the wood floor appeared an enormous pile of excrement!

Look again, Buddy," said the Dobermann.

This Turd is the accumulated Karma of your arrogant Leadership, which exploits and governs your country, and is transforming your great Land into a huge parking lot!"

The foul smelling Pile of Crap threatens to destroy you, if you come too close to it!"

127

The Images in his dream became more and more defined. He saw how the Pile became hard and dry, and broke up into pieces, some dry, and others still wet and evil smelling. These lay on a beautiful green athletic field.

Suddenly new life came to these pieces of fecal matter through a revolutionary bacterial culture as small hairy legs formed to become the basis of robot-like movements.

The Dobermann, sensing Johannes' disbelief, cocked his head to the right and asked: why are you so surprised"

That someone is corrupt?", it said with a deep, foreboding, and raspy voice.

That one sometimes falls prey to sensuous Temptations?"

The dark business world exists!"

Johannes, you have to grow up!"

The Dobermann was very proud of his knowledge of the human side of the world, it spoke further pompously;

To solve the problems of the world, which today are quite different than twenty years ago, one must wear several hats, do you know what I mean?"

First, you have to be aware of your health. That means you must always be fit to carry out the spiritual and physical tasks that remain before you. Faith is indispensible for the internal self; it can move mountains!

But I am not a Monk!"

Quite the contrary! But more on the order of the teachings of

Zarathustra, Kant and other real philosophers, which really take to heart the worth of the individual!"

You must arm yourself, because the End is coming!"

Your beautiful wife laying next to you, aren't you going to protect her? She loves you so much!"

The father of your wife, who still lives in the old states of Germany, has he wasted his life?"

What do you mean by that?" replied Johannes.

Nowadays your Top Dogs" routinely raise their hind legs on their employees: wages go down, they take away the health insurance and pension benefits, and send the jobs overseas."

Also, the greedy CFO's continue to piss mightily on the heads of the shareholders via fatter paychecks and benefits. Naturally in good and bad economic times they continue to enrich themselves unjustly!"

The american executives, and their top bankers, and regulators are an exclusive Nest of Snakes, a sneaky Group of men and women focusing on petty jealousy running amok, they are neither courteous nor polite in their actions."

Johannes began to sweat again. Alischraga began to snore, but lightly, not loud.

The Dobermann fixed his gaze on him, he saw the pearls of sweat on his rather large forehead.

Perhaps he would have an influence on him, at least divert his attention, he wanted to disturb him, in order to change his situation.

Johannes didn't know who the Dobermann was, for what reason was he interested in me? Is he a ghost? Is he a fallen angel? WHO IS HE?

The insects and the rats are taking away your home?"

He turned his head to the left, and spoke: Johannes do you like the Bible? If so, have you read Daniel 12:4?"

You should! The resurrection of the Dead!"

In these days, it is very dangerous for you and Alischraga, unless you recognize the signs!"

Johannes was totally dumbfounded, confused, and actually a bit angry.

Is he friend or foe?

Don't sleep, Johannes!"

Dream more! Are you drinking in more of my Images?"

Take the Bible in your hand and pay attention to the page on which Daniel 12:4 is!"

Johannes did what the dog wanted him to do. He read out loud to which the Angel said: keep it a secret, what I have now said to you; write it down, and seal God's Book, it is the last time it is opened!"

The dog suddenly began to be transformed into something else; it screamed obscenities, when it became a huge brass-plated Sphere.

The Sphere rolled around on the smooth wooden floor, gained

speed, bounced against the south wall of the bedroom and came to a stop.

It could speak. The Sphere grinned at me, then its external coating fell off, only the structure of the once gleaming Sphere remained.

Johannes perspired more, while Alischraga still slept.

He wondered now if the condition of his life would quickly go south?"

Then the skeleton became a woman, which thinks it is a candidate for President of the USA!

To make this point clear, she dressed herself elegantly and always wore red pumps with medium high heels. She offered an aesthehic, symmetrical muscularity and her gait resembled a well bred race horse. Her cinnamon brown skin made her extremely attractive.

Each hand carried colt 45 pistols, she spoke clearly and softly, so that her beautiful red lips could be advantageously displayed. She lured the public into her Spell.

Next to her stood a giant Greyhound dog. Was this a symbol of her unfaithful male companion? The Greyhound is certainly not a sheep dog, she mused.

Astonishment was not an understatement.

When he resisted her demands to touch her upper thighs, it laughed loud and lustily at him. „You Idiot! You dare to not come closer to me?"

Suddenly Johannes saw a flood of US Dollars pour out of her mouth!

I am making it possible for you to incentivize yourself to have more money!"

The Greyhound repeated her sensuous message, It barked unrelenting.

Johannes looked more closely at her sensuous rounded mouth, it poured out more money and, now credit cards!

Also plastic money? A huge amount, like Plankton in the sea which the sharks gladly ate!

Meanwhile she continued to spit out the mixture of money and credit cards. From three sides of her mouth; she smoked a cigarette, pot, and took cocaine, her red painted lips quivered ecstatically.

An enormous pile of US$100, 50, 20 Bills and credit cards lay on the finely polished wood floor, they reeked of rose flower petals.

Afterwards she spoke a difficult to understand Gibberish, that consisted on average of 6 to 7 Advertisements, which happen punctually during the 5 minute pauses in an american TV show.

"And who of all of you fools of the american TV culture, would no longer absorb the Propaganda?"

"No wonder that you all have no idea that you are now sitting in Shit!"

"Only empty phrases define the stupid Stuff!"

"Idiot!" screamed again the Creature at him: "you have caused a Hail Storm of baffling sentences and parts of sentences."

"Early morning time is golden, early bird always catches the worm!"

The female Creature shouted, cleared its throat, scratched the floor with her fine manicured toe nails, looked forward and backwards, shifted herself to the front and back, then licked Johannes' face and whispered in his ear:

"The country lives from hand-to-mouth, income is no longer assured."

Johannes observed the two black birds sitting on each of her shoulders, they flapped their wings, before it again spoke:

"Inflation concerns are spreading, innovation is needed, investment opportunities appear..."

"Stability?" "No!" "Volatility?" "Yes!"

"If one knows too much in advance, it spoils the surprise!"

"Abnormal?" "No." "Only the Experts!"

"Alcohol, Drugs, Tobacco, Weapons...they please me greatly!" "They keep me alert! It tingles me!"

This time she laughed long and lustily.

"The Sun's rays give me strength!"

"My door is always left open, if only cracked a bit."

"Forwards, backwards...."

"Neglectful tendencies are present in the world."

"Straight to Hell they come!"

"You are very nice, said the businessman." Which one?

"Racially motivated? Or the loosely enforced procedures of a government?"

"A high degree of individualism and Discipline!"

"Troublemaker, get out!"

"The devastating Forecast, I am optimistic, there is no recession here."

"They so correctly enjoy the sunny Life!"

"The Bank simply had bad luck!" „The poor top management!"

"The Careers would come to an End?"

"The beautiful Life no more?"

"My children at the private school no more?"

"Advice for my children from top management at this large bank no more?"

"I mean, what would I now do during the day?," scream the Wall Street men and women who once wore the most fashionable suits and skirts.

"These Shitheads are finally getting what they deserve!"

She readjusted the lipstick on her thick moist lips, and said: "especially the Regulators! These cowards, who received the bold advice from the Texas Senator, consisted of empty words which were at the heart of the GLB, led unavoidably to the Sub Prime Disaster!"

"And these *Fucking Know it Alls* followed the same erroneous advice!"

"They were duped by their own Greed!"

"They bought in to the concept of securitized investments and these other *smoke-filled collateralized debt obligations.*"

"Diversification of many weak borrowers was not a spreading of the risk! The ratings agencies should have known better. The valuation models indicated the risk in various tranches – AAA, AA, BBB, C, etc. which was not sufficient to hold default risk to acceptable levels."

The Creature: „The Models never fit real life, like me!"

"And, you know what, Johannes?"

"That Idiot, "Foreclosure Phil" - a derisive nickname for him, because the the Gramm. Leach, Bliley Act (GLB) served to create rapid innovation of financial instruments (CDO's, MBS', etc.) which led to massive mortgage defaults and huge loss reserves of the most "exclusive" banks!"

As she continues to spout off various obscenities, she slowly spread her legs to position herself like a cabaret dancer, and kick these high in the air, and said: "The yuppie Party King from Texas wants to always enjoy the sunny side of Life!"

"He and his mouthpieces revel in their appeasing language, which cause the dumb americans to fall into a deep slumber. They try to spread their pollen dust worldwide!"

"Of course, this Jerk, is largely responsible for the immense investment losses sustained by some of the largest prestigious banks in the world!"

The eyes of this woman, the American presidential candidate, were filled with rage. She said: „we wait gladly for the economy to improve!"

"But one doesn't need to climb off the hamster wheel, we need the cheap goods on the shelves!"

"Nothing must remain on the shelf!"

"One always imagines they are under pressure!" She laughed again and again!

That statement really bothered Johannes. How could this person be so insulting to the average Mary and Joe that are struggling to make ends meet?

The Creature's voice took on a southern tone, as it said: „Stay awhile, you are so purrrty!"

"Johannes, it is essential, that you experience this! Just now it is very important!"

"Pay attention!"

"Time is very valuable and will be more so in this Society!"

"Confusion rules the Globe, the Dollar Euphoria has vanished!"

"The War showplace and the enemy are not clearly identified!"

"Think, think, Johannes, who will stir up more volatility?"

She stared at him for several minutes, and said: "For us, clouds of smoke destroyed the most important message, and a normal Life!"

"Johannes, your Laptop is the Enemy!"

"This fashionable Apparatus, all those trendy cell phones, serve only to increase the global toxic trash pile!"

"Dirty Secrets of men, which sit in the most modern glass and steel buildings, create annually 25 to 50 million tons of toxic metals!"

"Progess? "Should one subtract this disgrace from GDP?"

"None of the bribed top level politicians would consider this idea."

"A different kind of toxicity existing in some American cities, provides sanctuary to the illegal immigrant, who jumps the line of people waiting to become citizens the legal way."

"The toxic atmosphere increases as the police are not permitted to question a person's legal status; to do that would be discriminating to the interests of the illegal immigrant, who competes against middle class citizens for better jobs!"

"Yes, yes, Johannes, everything nowadays has become so "fucked up!"

After her tirade, she breathed heavily, then she sat on the wood floor – she looked tired. She laid her skirt next to her, she wore no underwear. She tried to entice him.

Again he questioned the meaning of this mind-numbing dream. Frustrated, he wondered how he should react, if at all?

"Johannes, do you know that Senator who tried to burden the regulators with useless Regulations?"

"Good. Because he is a "Bitcher." Loose rules and vague interpretations since the Reagan years, he produces more Glitter than Reality."

Johannes thought that she had something new in her Head. On what basis does she want me to talk about this confusing Mess? Or is she simply a Ghost?

Then came the unholy Mess! About this Johannes had no Inkling! The Creature told him about Alistair's Conspiracy to control certain Health Aspects of the world's population!

"Johannes, you sleep very well when you dream about me," she said.

"And your beautiful wife still sleeps, she is so sweet."

"She perceives Nothing."

"She doesn't feel your movements on the mattress."

"Your Restlessness disturbs her not!"

"Enough of that." "Your boss is a crook, you have to protect yourself from him!"

"He will have you killed! "His Brazilian Wife plans your death, because she has a lot to lose."

"The Conspiracy was on September 11, 2001 set in motion!"

"On this day you try to save your life; you would have noticed *something unusual,* I mean, aside from the collapse of the WTC."

"Salmonella outbreak from Mexico?!"

"Tomatoes, Peppers, Parsley, Strawberries, Eggs...."

"E-Coli bacteria..."

"The politics of fear set in motion the idea of security of the world's Food Supply to assuage cleverly the panic stricken public, and that the people must be protected at all costs!"

"Irradiated beef from Brazil!" "Leaf lettuce irradiated!" "And wrapped in fine pink colored plastic!"

"For two years on the shelf and these contents remain Fresh!"

"Progress?"

"With this technology no one needs the regulators or consumer safety agencies!"

"Free trade benefits all consumers!" No more barriers to trade at the border!" "Let the good times roll!"

"Yeehaw!" Yells the old former President from West Texas as he strums wildly the strings of the guitar.

"The big banks have great plans! With your money, of course!"

She licked Johannes on the left cheek, she loved the taste of his sweat.

She wanted to crawl inside him; to touch his internal clock and its moving parts.

"Johannes, the truth is not always pleasant: the Regulators have really dropped the ball!"

ADRIAN VOGT

"They are unorganized and disorderly; they can't help themselves!" They don't want to support your endeavors, because you are more competent than they are!"

Alischraga awakend, looked at her man. He had screamed Something. Again and again.

"No, No! It can't be! You were a dead child that the Clinic burned up. You had no Mother!"

"Or you had been sold by that Psychiatric Clinic!"

He was quiet. He scarcely breathed. His forehead wet, and the temples red and hot.

"You are soaked in sweat throughout, what is the matter?"

He nodded his head to her and replied: "The same dream continues to haunt me!"

"I feel very uptight, something Evil is chasing me!"

He muttered: "Who is carrying the burden of this national disgrace?" The middle class is taking it all in!"

He thought of that Advertisement of a well known German Brewery - "Enjoy the taste, naturally with responsibility!"

Yes, to be responsible. Or does one have to be compelled to be responsible?

MORE ABOUT THE INSIDER

Johannes thought quite a bit about George Orwell's Belief that in a time of general misdirection a *revolutionary action is to speak the truth.*

Also, to act responsibly during these times is also "revolutionary."

In his rather roomy work station Johannes leaned back in his conventional swivel chair and held in his large hand a business card of a major player in the global markets.

For several minutes he occupied himself with the embossed print on the card, and it appeared to be slanted, tending toward the left side of the card!

Of course, one could still read the information, which referred the correct contact person with this giant global firm.

To be sure, this card did not look right; if received through the mail how would he or she perceive this rather unrefined card?

Since the firm is a big player in the industry, would the recipient think ill of the firm? A good question!

In any case, one might ask whether the not so exact production of this card is a sign of the arduous times in which we live, where one has to be content in general with items indicating a lesser quality, or at least, large amounts of mass produced items need not be perfect in style and substance.

It disturbed him that no one with the bank or the producer of the cards discovered this printing error.

Who was responsible for production control? How should he or she explain this mistake?

But it should not be surprising to him that that this situation exists, since it indicates that this bank and others operate just outside the law of common sense.

1995 was the year in which the large banks recognized that the Federal Statutes were less stringently observed than those of the states. Therefore, most of the national banks are supervised by the Office of the Comptroller of the Currency ("Nationalbank Authorities").

Also the OCC needed no oversight from the Congress to deal with its multi-million dollar budget. Besides, the OCC receives about three-fourths of its financial means from the regulated banks.

Of that, the public does not realize the "glaring" conflict of interest, and the OCC does not always receive prompt payment from its "client" banks.

"Man, that's hard to swallow, Johannes!" said the Bulldog who belonged to the same fitness club.

Johannes explained to him his concern, actually his extreme worry because of the radically changed Supervisory Direction of his management, which, in reality has led to a Policy of Disrespect for the laws and guidelines of the banking authorities.

THIS PICTURE DOESN'T HANG STRAIGHT

His colleague had long recognized this type of Arbitrage of different regulatory statutes, which gradually caused the team much concern.

The Leadership of the OCC surrounded itself with clever people that wanted cooperation with the bankers to somehow make it easier to conduct business utilizing methods that might skirt the rule of law!

Johannes tried to understand this line of reasoning, and said: "And also, you are aware that the OCC not only receives from the banks their "protection money", but the taxpayer finances the Agency."

"The Treasurer of the United States, the former Board Chairman of Goldman Sachs, oversees these National Bank Authorities."

"What do you mean-Protection Money?"

Johannes sighed and said: "the National Banks – Citi, Bank of America, etc., pay, annually to the agency, fees which cover the costs of examinations and other related expenses, which include those of the OCC offices maintained at each of the nationally chartered banks."

"Oh yeah," whispered JD.

"I remember well, how BofA, Riggs National Bank, and Wells Fargo were connected to various money laundering schemes."

"Were the banks punished?"

Johannes said: "Nothing official, only fines of a few million dollars."

"Why not?"

143

ADRIAN VOGT

"The cheating and trickery associated with the political Elite seeps through the imposing structure of the powerful decisionmakers."

"Like genuine Wormwood, the negative vibrations echo throughout an immoral structure and lead to its ultimate collapse.

"Oh, yes, so it is."

Johannes und JD turned again to the next set of machine leg presses. A geniuine competition developed between the two, as they breathed deeply to perform the last of 15 repetitions, so that they, with their fully extended legs could place the 500 pounds of weight to the beginning position.

The sweat dripped from JD's face as he said: "I heard Alistair and Fernanda discuss both Board Chairmen – predecessor and successor, they opined: both were idiots!"

"They discussed also the farce of the inflation indicator – core inflation, since this indicator did not include the volatile food and energy costs."

"The idea developed under Herb Stein, Head of the Council of Economic Advisors under President Nixon during the 1970's."

"Stein joked:" when a large amount of negative economic data on food and energy prices was deducted from the Consumer Price Index, then there might be little inflation!"

Johannes: "Nowadays the FRB reports such Crap."

"Not so bad, said the Chairman, as he presented the numbers recently before the Congress."

144

THIS PICTURE DOESN'T HANG STRAIGHT

Johannes noted that the Chairman did not mention the "true" circumstances behind the real estate Debacle.

Johannes likened the crisis to a swelling **carbuncle,** a red, swollen, and painful cluster of pus filled **boils** that are connected to each other under the skin. **Carbuncles** are more likely than **boils** to leave **scars.**

Of course, the rotten Pus of the Carbuncle burst; the rotten mortgage assets threatened to take down the entire financial system, but the pressure valve – the tight skin holding the enormous boil in place prior to bursting, now became flacid and flabby.

Examples of economic flabbiness - Negligence, Indifference, Apathy, and plain Laziness set the standards for the Nation, so that others could gradually follow the daily machinations of the political Elite to promote the ideas of a cooperation-filled global society. We could become a great, loving global family!

Bullshit!

The **scars** of the economic devastation linger a long time. For the clever insider, financial opportunities surfaced!

For they had the advantage of working very closely with the details – ah yes, the nuts and bolts of the economic disaster now being hastily reviewed by some of your elitist representatives in the Foggy Bottom City on the Potomac.

This time, they are reading thoroughly the stacks of legislation designed by their lobbyists to prevent another "Great Recession!"

JD and Johannes recalled that evening in August 2008, still wet with sweat from their regular workout, and listened to the news items emanating from the TV set fastened to the wall of the adjoining weight room of the Bally's health club: "S&P, Moody's

145

and Fitch are being interviewed to determine their role in the nascent developing Credit Crisis."

"The Greed for more and more fees allowed the Rating Services to review and participate in the design of complex financial structures to provide assistance to the Investment Banker, according to the experts."

"A higher return from a AAA rated complex transaction stood in stark contrast to conventional bonds of Corporations, Banks and sovereign entities with the same rating, that paid lower rates of interest to its investors."

"Certain Investors feel swindled, because they are only allowed to purchase AAA bonds, since the SEC – the Securities Exchange authorities – they permit the ratings from the Services, so that Funds managers can include the highly rated securities in their numbers."

"A Hedge Fund analyst opined: "two kinds of AAA instruments are differentiated."

"The conventional bond portrays higher market liquidity and lower risk of default; the newly structured bonds, which are securitized – passed on to the end investor, exhibit only limited liquidity."

"The Rating Services and the Banks had really "screwed up", as the huge losses from these new fashionable Asset Backed Securities (ABS) were not predicted by the quantitative risk management models; the so called Gurus estimated poorly the default risk!"

Johannes aud JD had not thought that the market turbulence would linger – but it did, for many months!

In the meantime, the year 2010 yielded few details on the transformation of the country into somethings else – as echoed by the new President.

However, some things do not change.

Finger pointing, the blame for the Debacle, yelling and shouting and hand wringing behind the heavy customized wooden doors of the legislative offices would eventually bring opportunities for some.

In the case of elected officials-information on expected legislation and lucrative government contracts can cause companies' securities to rise and fall within very short periods of time.

Aistair's connections to certain top congressional representatives led to enormous trading profits. Hefty returns based on access to insider information is illegal for the average citizen, but perfectly legal for elected officials!

In 8 IPO's, Alistair cashed in with his contacts; in the Visa transaction, legislation that would have hurt credit card companies, was withdrawn, the share price jumped from $44 to $64 in two days!

Undisturbed by the rules, he previously bought 5,000 Shares.

Since 2009, Johannes and the members of the team had already scattered in different directions, not too dissimilar from the actions of a covey of Quail that took flight after the hunters had discharged their 12 Guage shot guns at them.

Honest endeavors reportedly occupied the time of the team.

Johannes sported a different look. He would not be recognized.

JD loved the art of lifting anything heavy, as he called it.

His undercover work included driving a concrete pour truck with the logo – Big Johnson – on each side of the large lumbering vehicle.

Bittersweet Emotion

Johannes sported a mustache not too different from that of an average looking Middle-Eastern type. With that new look he could not be easily spotted in a crowd.

It was early morning of that day, his thoughts tumbled around in his head, not unlike that of a clothes dryer set on high heat.

He yearned for a return to simpler times: a handshake could conclude a contract without the necessity for various documents and a lawyer to secure the "deal."

Yes, indeed, he mused: one always felt good with honesty, and it costs nothing!

Even negotiations at large Forums, say, like the United Nations, to resolve national conflicts, could be handled in a simpler, more honest manner. The possibilities for such could be great; however, upon further reflection, not a likely scenario.

Or has life become so "lascivious" that one must expect the activities of Satan to plan, complicate, and confuse mankind?

Also, why has everything become so convoluted and serpentine?

Satan!

ADRIAN VOGT

Do the promises of the Elite consist of smoke and mirrors? Are they empty promises?

One of the best examples of dishonesty run amok would be the gradual theft from the American Social Security Trust Fund.

It didn't start out that way. The idea to dip into the Fund to cover "other expenses" of the Federal Government began small, take a little at a time! Leave a few IOU's to replace the drawdowns.

Both political parties are guilty of this "extreme immorality."

During the 1980's the Fund recorded enormous surpluses – the increasingly well paid middle class worker's contributions would be there held in trust, so the purpose of the Social Security Act of 1935 – it created a basic right to a pension in old age and insurance against unemployment.

The middle class flourished during this time period.

Sometime in 2010, a small deficit in the Trust Fund appeared.

Johannes mused: it wasn't hard to figure out "the whys and the wherefores."

Offshoring of jobs; the higher middle class tax revenues were now replaced by lower taxes paid into the Fund by the service industry worker.

America was no longer a manufacturing power as it once was! The plunderers – the elitist political and corporate class had their way with us!

Johannes' face began to swell with rage.

This shortfall received little attention from the public; the elite, of course, wanted to let sleeping dogs lay!

Except for the "laid off" middle class worker, including those of labor unions, the Press covered this dishonesty in the back pages of newspapers and magazines. No front page nonsense, the political elite would harbor in their thoughts – hopefully only a few honest people would notice this extreme immorality!

In short, a small deficit has become a large problem – thanks to the lack of restraint by both political parties to adhere to the original purpose of the Trust Fund!

They only thought of themselves – their careers funded by the tax payer!!

During this more than twenty year deceitful practice by the plunderers the public became drunk with their own stupidity as they were enticed by the pet projects of politicians claiming these would bring more prosperity to their community – on the taxpayer dime, of course!

They want to take other people's money for their own enrichment!

Others want to replace "earned benefit" with "entitlement."

The Trust Fund is just that – taxes paid into the Fund for the benefit of the worker – no one else's – only for the worker! Not for the politician or the chiselers!

Johannes and the team became "pissed off" over the progression of these events!

Miguelito Pohlmann, a Cuban refugee, spent quite a bit of time with Johannes and the team. At the time, Johannes did not know the full extent of devotion shown by Miguelito to the team and its principles of fair play.

Nor did Johannes realize his protective nature of Johannes and his Pakistani wife against the forces of evil.

"Were you aware of the plan of the global radicals to slowly destroy all people of European descent?"

"Life threatening for many of us, wouldn't you say?"

"The radical element wants to achieve more social diversity, so that a certain opaqueness in daily life comes about. Satan's objective, of course, is to confuse, block the light of radiant energy that emanates from a pure heart."

"Johannes, you are correct, these Shitheads believe in this concept."

"Yes, my skin color is light brown; that of your wife is darker."

"Identity politics uses the skin color as a political Cudgel to beat the opposition!"

Miguelito Uwe Pohlmann shows a beautiful mix of Cuban and german physical characteristics. His Mother, Angela, a Cuban native, met his Father, Ulrich, an East German, when he was stationed in Cuba.

After a few months' courtship, they married.

Miguelito explained that although his father was born in Erfurt and grew up there, he never had the opportunity to realize his dream of a fair and just Socialism in the German Democratic Republic (DDR).

Instead, he graduated from Engineering School in Erfurt as a Civil Engineer specializing in construction of Infrastructure.

He was commissioned in the late 1950's by the Batista Regime in Cuba to design and build up important sections of Cuban infrastructure; he worked closely with several American firms at the time.

After his commission with the East German regime was finished, he convinced his superiors that the family needed a vacation in the States.

On the condition of traveling to various major metropolitan areas in the U.S. to conduct certain undercover operations, the approval was given by his Chief in Erfurt; after arriving in Miami the family disappeared in to the Myriad of Cuban neighborhoods.

Minor plastic surgery and changes in dress enabled them to totally disappear from the communist regime.

Social security and passport documents with pictures of the "new" family members were issued by their new government.

Fluency in Spanish and English would further enable them to start new lives. Ulrich and Angela emphasized to Miguelito that "we are here to work and learn!"

In Early 1959, they re-located to Los Angeles, California to enjoy the "sunshine and orange juice."

Unfortunately, the boom in new construction and the rapid population growth led to a disappearance of orange and lemon groves in the outlying areas surrounding the City of Angels (LA).

The sweet smelling flowers of the citrus were replaced by concrete and businesses needing parking areas.

ADRIAN VOGT

However, several experiences were not pleasant for the Pohlmanns.

For example, that day in November 1959, when the neighbors had to move from their homes, because the City of Angels wanted their land in order to provide parking for the new Baseball Park.

Miguelito and his parents could not forget the Army of LA Sheriff's deputies forcibly removing those families who resisted the decision of the LA Board of Supervisors to provide **their** Chavez Ravine land for the new LA Dodger Stadium and parking facilities.

Some moments later a huge Kubota Bulldozer tore down the 40 year old houses, its heavy metal treads crushed the stucco and wood remnants into multi-colored pieces, a sort of mosaic paying tribute to the once proud neighborhood overlooking the expanse of once standing citrus groves, has now become an immense paved concrete parking lot.

The dust from the destruction of the development lingered in the air for several hours – years later the only dust in the area emanated from the thousands of cars arriving and departing the stadium area.

Now referred to as "Dodgertown," Senora Cantu related to the Pohlmann family: "have nothing against the baseball team, it is our team!"

With sadness in her voice, she brushed away the tears streaming down her still smooth cheeks, and finally cleared the lump in her throat, and said: "it is the way they did it, my mother, one of the most vigorous protesters against the removal of the once proud Chavez Ravine settlement, was dragged out of her house, she had a pistol in her left hand, she never used it."

154

The Deputies had no choice, said Senora Cantu.

Her mother was fined $500, and had to spend a month in jail.

The Cantu family no longer felt welcome. Had they made a mistake coming to America?

Some years later, the Emmerichs and the Pohlmanns became very close friends.

Johannes continued his discussion with him, while Miguelito was Hand drying the dinner dishes.

"Do you know that when one lays the dishes on the tablecloth, that the tiny drops from the damp plates, bowls, knives, forks, spoons remain, and gradually seep through the cloth, and these could remain awhile, before one observes that the tablecloth is once again dry?"

Johannes looked and waited for his reply. Somewhat confused, he replied: "Yes, but what's your point?"

"Similar to the drying process, is that the for many years commercial advertising through the mass Media, with the hope that their every five minutes break in the TV programs targeting certain consumer groups lead to increased consumption of their products!"

"This sort of brainwashing of the public exists!"

"A few networks can represent a certain viewpoint which may or may not focus on the common good of our country!"

"We live in dangerous times, Miguelito."

"We are slipping further into the Crisis!"

"The Crisis of our Identity is real: Satan is attempting to divide and overthrow our government, outside sources are compensating people to demonstrate against any attempt at Righteousness!"

"No one appears to want to return to the tried and proven Christian Principles of our Lord and his wonderful Son. Priase the Lord! Hallelujah!"

"I am speaking of a fresh voice to bring back the historical Blueprint for Success of a country."

"The Evil of past oppressive government Regimes is making a comeback"

Johannes stopped speaking suddenly. His face appeared frozen. He felt FEAR, he broke out into a cold sweat.

Alischraga recognized his condition, a form of Post Traumatic Stress Disorder (PTSD) he still was trying to overcome.

She quickly reached for his neck and trapezius muscles, rubbing them with her well formed strong fingers, up and down in smooth, short and long deep strokes.

After five minues, he began to relax and come out of his trance.

Alischraga said: "Miguelito, my Johannes has already been through a lot."

"We can continue the discussion later."

"No! We continue now, I am better," Johannes said with a strong and reassuring voice.

She was happy that he recovered so fast, he was making improvement, she thought.

"Miguelito, do you have more time for us?"

"Please, Johannes, let's talk more."

Johannes recovered from his short bout with the PTSD; more than likely from the toxic effects from the WTC collapse. But he knew IT would again return.

His face was no longer pale, his olive complexion, inherited from his Scottish Mother, began to fold over the ashen countenance.

"We are now experiencing more and more anti-social behavior, I believe because of the access globally now to the cable TV which enables viewers to observe the best and worst traits of the human race."

"Unfortunately the original purveyors of this technology belonged to THAT societal segment in West Germany during the early to middle 1980's, and they were very profit-conscious, to the extent of extreme exploitation, as in the days of the Jewish persecution."

"Images of extreme cruelty and questionable behavior exceeded the demand for good deeds and positive behavior."

Johannes felt his FEAR again beginning to well up within him, constricting his breathing; this time he tried not to show it. He continued the discussion, as the anxiety slowly ebbed away.

"And one of the largest producers of telecommunications equipment always stood before the door of the German government agency for the license and the accompanying financial assistance."

"Profit in the millions of Deutsche Marks was harvested through the total project to lay TV cable across the West German frontier."

ADRIAN VOGT

"The cable equipment firm President had the right credentials: Prussian Heritage, a high ranking German officer close to the "Fuehrer," and a close friend to the then Chancellor Helmut Kohl."

Johannes remembered this impressive financial victory for this self-centered family, which counted as one of the most influential of West Germany.

One of the sons, Benedict, who spent seven years in Brazil as the Representative of a prestigious – yet medium sized German private bank had befriended Johannes, and had great confidence in him for his business and regulatory acumen.

In reality, he relied on Johannes to handle many of his rather controversial projects – which others would not want to undertake for the favor of this person – some would even use that unkind word – Asshole, to describe Benedict.

"Johannes! "Come visit with me, please!" "I need another favor from you!"

"Be so kind to me and deliver this gift to my girl friend!"

Benedict grinned broadly at Johannes, and said: "For this favor, I am so appreciative to you!"

Johannes took the beautiful bouquet of flowers of varied colors from the credenza. He recognized the pungent Aroma – these appeared to have been flown in from Colombia.

Behind the dark colored vase, stood various framed photos of the family. Of particular interest was the picture of the Prussian Patriarch, in full Nazi uniform. His smile indicated a sort of self-centered individual obsessed with money.

Johannes strolled to his car, which was parked in the garage of the building housing several foreign bank branches on Brickell Avenue, climbed into his black Audi sedan, and drove down through three levels of parking spaces.

He turned left on to Brickell Avenue and drove to the prestigious Miami suburb of Coconut Grove. Within five minutes, as a result of light traffic at 3 PM, he arrived at his destination – the Grove Isle club.

At the guard gate, he greeted Jose, a mustachio and rather jovial type, and proceeded to the main entrance of this architectural Wonder – a twenty story Tower with sloping balconies forming a forty five degree angle where the elevators were positioned.

He climbed in the first floor eleventor and could observe the upward glass encased shaft to the top floor. He pressed the button to the twentieth floor. The elevator functioned smoothly to its destination. He stepped on thick off-white plush carpet as the elevator door opened.

On each side of the front door of apartment 202, multi colored tapestries of tropical flowers decorated the entire hallway.

He pressed the fine brass plated door bell only once. A rather tall and slender woman opened the door, and said: "Are you Johannes?"

Johannes replied: "Yes."

She was really pretty, he thought; medium length black hair, olive complexion, dark eyes which seemed to change color with certain lighting conditions, all attributes together, she exhibited soft tenderness.

She wore a conservative light colored pant suit and leather sandals. She was not flat chested.

She asked him to sit down – anywhere, as the large living space contained many pieces of well positioned furniture- the area reminded him of a very modern showroom in a trendy furniture store in Miami.

He sat down in one of several mini sofas.

Through two giant glass doors he saw a far reaching balcony, on each corner stood six foot tall Romanesque pillars which had on top exotic flower baskets. The humid, sunny mid-afternoon air provided sufficient moisture for these rather sensual-looking plants.

Then she said: "Johannes do you have something for me?"

He gave her the handsome bouquet which contained a letter addressed to her.

The shadow colored vases and fine cocktail glasses on the hanging glass shelves began to show different colors in response to the changing position of the sun.

She opened the envelope and slowly read the letter; she paused for several minutes, looked at Johannes, and calmly stood up from her mini sofa, walked to the nearest refuse container and placed the entire letter in it.

Her reaction was controlled before she said: "that Bastard!"

"I gave him seven years of my Life; he was the Love of my Life! He threw me away like a piece of trash!"

Then she moved closer to Johannes, and said: "You can stay awhile longer with me, if you would like to. It's O.K."

Johannes smiled at her, and said: "Perhaps later, until then."

He could feel her dark eyes following him as he walked through the threshold towards the elevator.

Benedict spoke of his relationship with Rosa when he was the Representative in Sao Paulo. Although from a very wealthy and influential family in Brazil, with many important connections in Brasilia, the Capitol, she would not fit in German society.

Her beautiful skin color, he reasoned, could be a negative for him as his family would not accept her.

"This could even impact my career at the private bank, actually stall potential promotions!"

"It had to be short and sweet, Johannes."

Johannes left his office with a very bad taste in his mouth.

He remembered Rosa's assessment of her jilted self. She became a throw away bottle that once contained the finest champagne – she was correct in her description of the contents of THAT letter.

At that time Johannes harbored the expectation that he would probably not meet her again. He would be wrong.

MASQUERADE

Johannes opened the door to the glass encased staircase to other floors and stepped on the threshold.

Fernanda was several steps ahead of him. She swung her broad hips to garner attention from others – especially the men.

What a piece of work, he thought.

Through the half opened door, he noticed his colleague, Simone von Tronchin in her office thumbing through a large file that contained the Compliance Guidelines of MPAG New York.

She turned around and waved Johannes into the room, and said:

"Johannes, the guidelines are seriously lacking in substance, and are very brief. In short, it appears as if someone simply threw together a bunch of memos over the years to show that a Compliance Manual does exist!"

"This is pure crap!"

"An organization Chart to indicate clearly the responsibilities of employees to monitor and enforce adherence to internal guidelines has not been found. A comprehensive Compliance Manual should include at the very least, "Know your Customer," Bank Secrecy and money laundering, insider trading, and conflict-of-interest. Also, financial accuracy and transparency of all operations within the institution is a MUST."

"The Branch has no compliance officer. The Branch Manager, the Head of Audit and the Manager of the Funds Transfer Department perform money laundering training!"

"In this pile of crap there is no mention of head office's role, who supervises overseas branch compliance, and how the activites are executed."

"In prior examination reports, before Alistair and Fernanda could purposely retire these reports, no one would ask that feared question: What did the prior examiners of the MPAG branch find out about employee compliance with internal operations!" questioned Johannes.

Simone didn't reply.

Outside of Johannes, no one completely uncovered this embarrassing mess.

However, the Branch Manager sensed a developing problem in this area and mentioned to the prior examiner-in-charge that "all would be taken care of!"

That was two years ago!

"With other major banks, I had never discovered such confusion, in my extensive review of this extremely important function!"

Johannes held his breath before he answered Simone. The first issue that he had to decide was whether her concerns were justified.

The prior two years' reports were not in the file room.

Johannes picked up the receiver and called the Executive Vice President.

"Hello." "Johannes, so good to hear from you," said Alistair.

"Yes, I have these reports."

"Please come by my office, and I will gladly hand these over to you."

"By the way, do you think there may be a major problem at the branch?"

"No, Alistair, I just want to tie up a few pending matters."

Johannes hung up and went to the 23rd floor.

He felt uncomfortable, something bothered him, perhaps a lingering thought which lurked in his subconscious.

"Johannes, come in."

Alistair grinned broadly, and said: "Only for your consumption, do I hand these over to you."

"Did you know that several of my closest buddies work at the Branch?"

"No, Alistair. But I look forward to meeting your pals".

"Well, O.K. Johannes."

"I am certain that you will do the right thing with this examination."

That was it, that was all he had to say, thought Johannes.

But the words: "you will do the right thing," disturbed him.

The examination reports of the prior two years were brief in content. However, there was an incredible amount of information in the Confidential Section of the report that gave him pause.

Especially in the area of swap activities, which was growing rapidly, and the processing of these transactions were delayed, sometimes for days!

He asked Simone where were the new product reviews and the policies and procedures related to the Swaps business line – nowhere to be found.

Simone was right in her critical assessment of the Compliance function.

The prior examiner had clearly recommended to the branch manager that not only the weak compliance issues but other critical operational weaknesses be immediately addressed and resolved.

Unbeknownst to the examination department staff that performed a review of all reports prior to distribution to the supervised entity' management and the Board of Governors in Washington DC, Alistair had inserted certain language which in effect was to dismiss any urgent follow up of management's corrective actions!

Of course, the Branch's management ignored the advice of the examiners.

As a result, since the last examination, the unsatisfactory operations environment had not improved.

Johannes knew that Alistair and Fernanda, with the blessing of the tenth floor residing President of the Fortress, could now begin to develop closer relationships with the Wall Street Executives.

Johannes did not like this change in approach with bank management – a kinder and gentler regulator, combined with the Colombia University professor's recommendations for "value added."

Neither did Alistair like the recommendations of that "fat fuck," but he went along with the new trend since he could profit handsomely from any regulatory action approved by the Congress through his insider contacts in the house and the senate.

Johannes needed a break, arose from his leather upholstered swivel chair and entered the dark TV room. He observed the speech of the new incoming President who promised to transform the America that we know.

He emphasized the failure of certain voter groups to recognize the needed changes in one's thinking about the directon the country should take: in the state of Pennsylvania he chastised the individuals that hold dear to their heart their religious freedoms and gun ownership.

Miguelito heard the same speech. "People never learn," he sighed.

Others, particularly in the Media, gushed over the new President's promise to promote a "Sense of Fairness"for all and address the issues of social injustices and irresponsibility."

However, others became impatient with the hours long pontificating about the elimination of Greed and the heralding of a new Era of Responsibility and Transparency in Government.

Tina, an executive Vice President, Head of Capital Markets

and Economics Departments, also occupied the tenth floor of the Fortress. She liked the speech for the first one hundred days of the new administration.

She harbored the thought of greater insider trading within the new administration and the FRBNY. She had seen this situation before in 1998.

In appearance, she appeared quite stout, her long hair touched her broad shoulders, but the hair style always seemed to resemble that of twenty years ago.

Johannes looked at the stringy and rather oily hair. Perhaps she used a different color shampoo, or hadn't washed it in several days.

As she watched the speech, her reading glasses hung at an angle on the lower part of her nose.

She screamed inwardly with Delight, as she listened further to his Message of Hope: finally we are one diverse society. WE finally made it possible that HE is now OUR President.

Unfortunately, Tina views almost everything through rose colored Lenses, she tended toward viewing most things in a positive manner.

Kinda like other politicians who assured the public, as they reached further in their pockets to fund their careers in government, that everything is **gonna be awl riiight.**

Of course, few would even dare to question the political correctness of the new Management headed by"Big Bill."

She did everything to please Big Bill, who also wanted positive **Outcomes** and Results in examination reports, complex analyses, forecasting, new products, and research reports.

However, her zealous pursuit of positive results led frequently to an internal panic situation for her underlings as her perceived zeal for her objectives are rewarded quite nicely, as long as one agreed with her assessment!

A fan of Big Pharma was, in her case, not exaggerated: her rather corpulent physique led to low energy levels, mood swings, blotchy skin, thinning hair, diabetes, and high blood pressure, which caused her to use several prescribed medicines to control these shortcomings in her overall health.

Her diet was terrible: Tina could not resist the appeal of fast food, the many overly processed foods of the factory farmer and giant processed food companies, it was so tempting, she mused.

As Executive Vice President, she could pretty much do what she wanted, especially with matters related to trading so-called innovative capital market instruments, since few of her management colleagues knew "Zilch" about these new products.

As a former head of trading at MPAG, she knew the weaknesses of operations controls and management's inclination to begin trading new instruments as soon as possible – the back office can always catch up to the confirmation of contracts, sometimes, a week behind – but no matter, the staff was very experienced, they did not need to be told what to do - because the bank management poached these experienced individuals from other trading firms that housed their operations in the canyons of Wall Street.

She openly stated: "We don't need burdensome operations manuals and compliance rules to tell us what to do. Instinct tells them what and how to do it."

Tina and her team viewed the tragic events of 9/11 as nothing unusual – shit happens, replied Tina to her other colleagues.

This Picture Doesn't Hang Straight

They did not panic like Fernanda.

From the tenth floor of the Fortress, she could only see the clouds of gray and black dust hovering over the site appearing like huge dark gray ghosts.

She and her team, wearing protective masks from the dust coming through the heating and air conditioning systems, walked calmly in to the long hallway.

Sometimes, the emotions of the moment caused them to race down the hallway, bouncing against the walls on their way to safer floors.

When asked: "don't you worry about the air quality when outside and commuting to your home?"

"No. Because Rudi said the wind favored us, it propelled the fine particles of still burning materials upward, a sort of whirling circular action, so to speak, into the atmosphere"

Alistair smiled. He knew the Governor of New Jersey would parrot the same Crap.

In the meantime, Johannes and Simone continued their search for the new product review concerning credit derivatives that supposedly function as a backstop to asset backed securities.

They remembered their heated discussion with the Branch manager, Markus Brunner, about the perceived credit quality of asset backed securities, which total portfolio at the branch increased rapidly, averaging increases of ten percent annually.

The mathematical modelling employed would predict the degree of default by the borrower, reiterated Markus.

ADRIAN VOGT

However, Markus admitted that some at head office questioned the liquidity of such instruments and the necessity to hold reserves for potential default of borrowers within the tranches, in case quantitative models under estimate default risk.

Simone and Johannes noted the difference in liquidity between the asset-backed security and conventional bonds.

Also, no formalized new product review could signify that relevant personnel at the branch might have been involved in the assessment of market, liquidity, credit, revaluation and model risks, and the role of operations, accounting and legal issues may not be fully understood.

Johannes and Simone left Markus' office on Park Avenue and caught the subway train to their downtown location near the gigantic still smouldering hole where the proud and majestic World Trade Center once stood.

The whirr and grinding of excavation equipment and dump trucks leaving and entering the area could be heard blocks away.

They entered their office building and went to the 23rd floor where Dan Steinmetz had his office.

Dan, a tall, well dressed Man with blond hair, and extremely brilliant in matters pertaining to credit default swaps and other similar derivative products, was packing his personal items in a large briefcase.

He greeted them, and said: "I can't work with that person anymore! She is so incompetent and unbending in her views on these new products."

We looked at each other in disbelief and then nodded to him to continue his complaint.

THIS PICTURE DOESN'T HANG STRAIGHT

We discovered that Tina, his superior, had asked him to fully research the advantages and disadvantages of marketing and booking the credit default swap (CDS), followed with his views on how to account for this "below the line" product.

Dan replied: "I worked on this damned project for more than two years after the adoption of GLB of 1999 and those worthless risk focused procedures."

Dan had also consulted with one of the influential members of the Board of Governors in Washington D.C. who warned against the marketing of the CDS and its application as a back up of asset backed securities launched in the capital markets.

He said: "robust monitoring and review of all assets – mortgages, loans, other types of assets used as collateral to ultimately serve as the "take out" on repayment of securities must be a substantial part of any examination of a major bank in this developing market place."

Also, discretionary sampling of mortgage and loan portfolios will not suffice."

Johannes and Simone sighed loudly, and asked the question: "who will invest the time to check out all collateral to determine its ability to repay investors at maturity? Or maintain principal and interest payments as contracted?"

Dan mentioned to Tina that the CDS should be classified as an insurance contract between two parties, one of whom is providing insurance or a "take out" for the repayment of the securities of the lender if the financial entity or corporation fails to satisfy its obligations.

Tina knew that the seller of the insurance protection receives a fee for its contractual obligation to make whole the purchaser of the contract. She did not like the idea of this investment to be designated as insurance since all particpants – especially sellers would have to maintain reserves to cover its obligations over time.

As insurance, it must be regulated!

Tina: "No, No, our clients don't want to use any of their capital as a reserve!"

Dan: "And as a standby letter of credit to provide additional comfort to the purchaser and the marketplace?"

"It is nothing more than a contingent liability off the balance sheet of the seller, in many cases."

Dan could visualize the runaway speculation of the marketplace: a hedge fund could sell protection to a bank, which will resell the same protection to another bank, and such dealing will continue, he mused.

Tina accepted Dan's analysis, but did not approve the classification of these derivatives as 'insurance."

Nor did she want to consider standby letters of credit as the fee income would likely not be as remunerative as that from over the counter derivatives.

Dan was furious. His face turned beet red, as he further discussed Tina's unwillingness to classify these as insurance, instead the term "swap" enabled the seller to avoid regulation, no reserves from premiums of fees received to insure against future losses!

At that time the CDS market dwarfed the entire capitalization of all stock markets combined.

This Picture Doesn't Hang Straight

Dan was pleased to tell Tina to "bugger off" and left the FRBNY the next day.

Simone and Johannes were saddened by this de facto betrayal of the original objectives of the FRB System.

The rest is history, as Johannes recalled the gradual deterioration in examination effectiveness.

He mused about the once protective role of the American central bank as a creator of economic stability and full employment.

It would become very clear to Johannes that the respectable Central Bank had abdicated its responsibilities, as approved by the Congress of the United States.

Unknown to the majority of the American public, the Federal Reserve Bank's contract with the American people is now in practice "Null and Void."

Going forward, the central bank would basically pretend to be the guardian of the public interest.

Alistair continued to bark commands to other examiners from his opened door of the 23rd floor office, directly across from the "Fortress," about the necessity of culling "old" examination reports from the secured documentation filing cabinets – in reality, these could be accessible to anyone – particularly after hours to the few "ass kissers" hoping to impress their bosses with their after hours work ethic!

All they had to do was appear to be working!

Unfortunately, there was another purpose besides the streamlining of the file room. The removal of older examination reports served to cover up any glaring supervisory mistakes that

ADRIAN VOGT

could lead to accusations of favoritism for certain banks – now known privately as the clients of the FRBNY.

Compliance with the long standing "tried and proven" established examination procedures was now in jeopardy.

Going forward, the examiner could no longer perform "detective work" prior to an examination; a track record of potential non adherence to supervisory criticisms and corrective actions would not be as apparent.

Johannes and Alistair continued their conversation of the new risk focused approach and its potential for abuse.

It became clear to Johannes that this charade – at the behest of Alistair and Fernanda, began during 1995, when the clever central bankers talked up the necessity for "risk focused" reviews at their "client banks."

According to Alistair, the impetus of this necessity or a cleverly imposed charade emanated from a scathing rebuke of the central bank's strategy of "live and let live" or "maybe the problem will go away if we wait long enough," in a lengthy article in the New York Times dated October 19, 1995.

Another team of examiners had "dropped the ball" in connection with this major foreign bank's operation in New York City. They still had their jobs.

At the crux of the central bank's "Masquerade" that the regulator was actually doing something to protect the public interest was to introduce the Guidelines/Objectives of Risk –Focused Documents to allegedly supplement the already voluminous examination manuals, which every supervised bank since the early 1980's could easily access for operational control guidance.

174

THIS PICTURE DOESN'T HANG STRAIGHT

The new guidelines consist of "interrelated analyses"that map supervisory strategy.

Johannes and the team knew immediately that this was a "make work"project and a sham to cover career oriented individual's asses (CYA) in case something **too controversial** appeared in an examination report! Also, review examiners "did their number" on the examination report to make certain of the CYA nature of the new guidelines.

A result of the new approach was more work performed in the office of the FRBNY than at the examined bank!

The central bank's reluctance to intensify its reviews of adherence to internal policies and procedures, conduct verbal discussions with employees performing critical operations activities, review their daily work for accuracy and procedural conformity, list all concerns in the examination report – serious, not so serious, and those small infractions, that taken together, could wreak real havoc on a financial institution, began in October 1995.

Johannes noted that the new approach cautioned the examiners not to be "too prescriptive" for the action to be taken by management to correct operational weaknesses!

In other words, the central bank worried more about the reactions of management to the justified criticisms than the actual followup needed by bank management to quickly resolve the weaknesses to avoid supervisory actions.

Whew!

The new guidelines were really a postponement of corrective actions – the word soon got out that the FRBNY was becoming a "kinder and gentler regulator!"

175

Does that sound familiar?

The Team knew that to succeed in the field of regulation and, ultimately, law and order enforcement, one has to use the hammer on occasion.

Suddenly, Johannes' thoughts turned to those tragic events of September 11, 2001: he saw a different kind of rain, the wafting glass particles and toxic dust fell to the ground, and upon impact, some of it seemed to bounce lightly upward, and the cross winds formed huge clouds that climbed further and further in the Air.

Some of the unfortunate were covered with white ash, carrying their shoes, running barefooted through the clumps of ash.

Their lungs and skin took in the toxic poisonous air that blanketed the affected downtown area.

From left and right, came the rolling wall of black dust from the careening trucks and ambulances racing through the streets to their life-saving destinations – the terror stricken wounded pounded on the doors of the hospitals and these Guardian Angels hastily set up refuges from the terrorist attacks that caused Johannes to re-evaluate the causes of Terrorism – in all forms.

He began to believe that the underlying reasons were really quite simple: the common theme was the irregularity of unexplained things – what the clever people don't want you to know!

And this was Satan's plan to destabilize and confuse!

Johannes and his team would never give up in their struggle to uphold the principles of our Lord- Jesus Christ!

Quitting is not an option for a soldier in the army of the Lord!

The turning point for the dilution of regulatory action came in 2001 when all regulators – Finance, Agriculture and Big Pharma, were discouraged by the Elite to strictly enforce existing regulations!

The Charade was in full swing – the loosening of the enforcement action also included the reliance on the taxpayer to pay for all regulatory mistakes related to the supervision of the BIG THREE industries: Finance, Agriculture and Big Pharma.

The elitist politicians and their legislated regulators became the pawns of the BIG THREE.

They then could wear their finest Masquerade garb and enjoy their social parties with no end in sight! Viva la Vida loca!

A new crisis is now being planned by the women and men of the executive level at the BIG THREE.

The next crisis, like the last one ending effectively in early 2009, in terms of stock market recovery, would again rely on THAT very reliable source of funds – you guessed it: the tax payer. Once again, left in the lurch!

Why should anyone be surprised about this fact?

The freeloaders: illegal aliens, the elitist career politicians, and the Corporate Front First (CFF), whose strategy to bring all peoples of the world together via the BIG THREE - Finance, Pharma and Agriculture, would reap huge windfall profits GLOBALLY!

Well, yes.

The corrupted heirs of the original founders of the Federal Reserve System – represent the real power brokers.

The strategy was clear as fine glass, despite the daily Propaganda of the major Media concerns.

Their charade was easy to recognize, the Media changing often their message depending on who they are beholden to for their compensation.

The many times senseless behavior of these media "whores" in their fine Garb, could be traced to the manipulation by the CFF.

After digesting these mental revelations, Johannes left Alistair's office, and noted mentally that "red thread of abuse" of regulatory responsibility – the same "Rules of the Road" became the new Mantra of the SEC, FDIC, Department of Agriculture, Energy, FRB, OCC, etc.

Johannes and Simone recognized quickly that the trading in hard to understand derivatives totaling around $670 Trillion during 2008/2009 was behind the crisis.

The Trillions of Dollars bailout in 2009 of the participants led primarily to the bloated balance sheet of the FRB system, from $800 billion to ca. $4.3 Trillion in 2009.

Perhaps the most telling of all was the GLB Act of 1999 which replaced the Glass Steagall Act of 1932; the latter separated commercial banking and investment banking activities to prevent another speculative repetition of the Great Depression.

Also, the SEC allowed the leverage limitations on brokerage activities to be dissolved so that even more contingent liabilities and trading positions could be carried.

Special Purpose Subsidiaries within the Bank holding companies enabled more deriviatives – credit default swaps to be marketed and placed on the books of these subsidiaries —not visible to the casual reader of financial reports.

The Reserves for future defaults outside of the expected projected losses of the rating agencies (S&P, Moodys, etc.) were not provided for.

The Crisis was global, since the Rating Agencies' assessment of the bundled MBS was taken at face value instead of the major banks performing their own credit repayment analyses.

Unfortunately, betrayal of moral principles was part of the rising tide of global secularism and Johannes would soon be the focus of Satan's messengers.

Charade Maximized

Johannes had heard many times that a company head is supposed to create a value system for the enterprise, and live by those values.

Even the so called new establishment management parrots this modus operandi.

O.K., but he also thought a system that does not protect the public from the vagaries of untruths, and fails to observe the greatest rules of life – the Ten Commandments and the penchant for observing the Golden Rule: treat others the way you would want them to treat you, is a tool of the Corrupter, who encourages a Netherworld type of value system.

Johannes knows that Satan always creates an atmosphere of confusion and doubt which corrupts one's abilities to be a better person.

Johannes remembered his rendering of a scene in his mind that showed his near term future. It wasn't pretty for him and his beautiful Alischraga.

But he also recalled the machinations of that creature in his dreams that appeared to foretell certain negative events.

The longer he looked through the credit files of the very largest members of the CFF, the more convinced he became that there

180

THIS PICTURE DOESN'T HANG STRAIGHT

is always a driving force, an underlying reason for something to happen.

He came gradually to the conclusion that some of the Executive level women and men of the CFF were involved in the new Charade, even endeavoring to maximize this strategy. And they did not want to be deterred from their efforts.

Their strategy for the downside of political risk was to engage in the lobbying effort with the "in their pocket politicians on both sides of the aisle,"so to speak, to protect their interests: the availability of taxpayer funds to counter any strategic shortfalls – in this case, cash flow and the creation of shareholder value.

It was a society which Alistair, Rosa and Fernanda were active participants. They always wanted to create a respectable appearance at any meeting with the press relating to rating agency presentations.

Johannes and his team did not share the idea of a continued exploitation of the middle class taxpayer – at least, he thought that all team members, as taxpayers, would reject that notion.

Another credit file caught his eye, the analysis of loan repaymemt for this very large food processor reflected sparse details – he could only find a terse memorandum of credit department acceptance of the AAA Rating given by the Rating Agencies!

Johannes was enraged that in most cases the MPAG New York branch had not performed its own analyses of credit worthiness and potential default risk!

Bill questioned the rationale of relying on Rating Agency data as a substitute for the credit department's evaluation.

181

The credit department analysts opined that this procedure resulted in significantly lower cost for the branch – New York was proud of its position as the most profitable in the overseas network.

Well, O.K.

The false information conveyed to the financial markets via misguided incompetence – became endemic among all major global banking entities.

Johannes mulled over in his mind that false assessments of Rating Agency ratings of mortgage backed securities and other similar instruments went back to 2002, and at that time his team did ask the right questions and the controversial answers given by the branch were detailed and identified in the examination report as serious operational weaknesses.

Supervisory action consisted of management's correction of examiner concerns within six months, were presented to Alistair and Fernanda for their review and approval before passing on the Report to the tenth floor.

Johannes and his team understood now the reluctance of their tenth floor management to fully examine the credit commtiments and their usage by the major money market banks and their overseas universal business banks – they were afraid of what would be found if the return to a policy of thorough examination of all assets at their "client banks" was carried out!

Were they also afraid of the investing public's reaction to a "real time" evaluation of underlying book values of major banks worldwide?

It was becoming easier to understand the rationale behind the GLB Act of 1999. Under the Umbrella of the FRB the "client banks" and their securities operations could be examined by the other regulators and these results copied to the Board in Washington DC.

Less direct scrutiny by Johannes and his team meant more cost control because of LESS time spent on site at the "client" bank.

FRB system decision makers wanted NO PROBLEMS to deal with, to make absolutely certain that all of their client banks and subsidiaries demonstrated at least a "satisfactory" financial condition!

Their supervised entities must be decribed as maintaining a "copasetic" control environment and minimal challenges to their asset quality.

In other words, if necessary, turn a blind eye to risky business activities of the largest members of the CFF, and "if things go south" rescue them with taxpayer support!

Somehow blame future crises on the Fog of Uncertainty and the human tendency to self destruct. To regulate more would somehow not prevent recessions, so the senior Oracle.

Johannes and the team felt very alone and discouraged, did they suddenly become a target of the forces of evil?

Was the Senior Oracle a Minion of Satan?

Johannes realized that he should not be naïve as to who Satan will use.

Satanic or elitist control over the regulatory environment relating to the Big Three was now clear.

The politically influenced Agricultural and Pharmaceutical

areas were no different than the atmosphere of lax financial regulation.

Johannes spoke loudly in almost the roar of an aggressive animal to the team: "that a reckoning within the big three will start with them, and they must be willing to undergo severe hardship, if required, to survive and ultimately push their own agenda forward! And, the reckoning will not end with them!"

"Our values will survive!"

"It is worth fighting for, even if it takes another generation to alter this corrupt and dangerous situation to individual sovereignty!

Our God is watching!"

It was 1800 hours. Workout time again.

Richard lifted the barbell overhead and performed triceps presses, emphasizing the large tricep head. He was achieving a good pump. Five sets of 15 reps.

He said: "The country is goin' to shit, you'll see."

"Life is fulla highs 'n lows, Johannes."

It was not unusual for the team to engage in regular exercise of some sort to relieve the buildup of adrenalin during the course of the day.

Some outbursts of raw emotion could boil over into rather coarse language and threats of retribution against certain management as well as those that "cozy up" to the guys and gals of the tenth floor.

It is now generally recognized that regular resistance training can bring a person to an optimal mental and physical condition.

He remembered that it was not always that way.

Most used their barbells at home – primarily distributed by York Barbell Company in York, Pennsylvania.

At that time, Joseph Weider was a protégé of Robert Hoffman, Owner of York Barbell and the USA Olympic Weightlifting coach.

Some of the very first health clubs originated in California and later in Texas during the 1950s.

Ed Yarick's gym in Oakland, California produced Steve Reeves, the 1947 Mr. America. All Mr. America Title holders since 1939 originated in the Golden State and the contest candidates made Muscle Beach a much revered workout facility.

Johannes, barely a Teenager in 1953, observed in the month of June how a Mr. America competitor, Malcolm Brenner, won an impromptu bench press contest – 50 continual strictly performed repetitions with 205 pounds, at Muscle Beach – the weather conditions were actually optimal at 1100 hours – 75 degrees Fahrenheit and sunny.

Even some world weightlifting records were attempted there – David Sheppard, of the US Olympic team introduced the squat style three Olympic lifts – military press, snatch and clean and jerk.

At that time the split lifting style was the most popular.

Johannes' memory of those days was superb, expressed the team members, most of whom now employ the squat syle of lifting.

As a pioneer in lifting to assist athletic endeavors, those early days were met with resistance- the use of weights was frowned upon – one could become "muscle bound!"

ADRIAN VOGT

In other words, one couldn't play football, run track, throw the shotput and discus, etc., effectively, because, somehow muscularity and strength impeded your ability to compete.

That Myth was soon disproved.

Of note, several world records in track events were set as a result of strength training; beginning in the late 1950's.

During the week the team was training for the third time; as usual, they focused on working out, and temporarily forgot their frustrations on the job.

However, on occasion, the "Job" was discussed during the workout, and they sensed an uneasy calm before the storm: thorough regulation of management of risk during an environment of political correctness at the FRBNY would be subordinated to the whims of their senior management.

They had to prepare themselves for the worst case: a further deterioration in the practice of enforcing standards of known "best practices" within the basic industries that deal with money and wealth, pharmaceutical and nutritional supplementation, and food processing and preservation.

How did the team know that the regulatory environment would be watered down across industry: the consultants on report writing were hired by the heads of all regulatory agencies: the SEC, FDIC, FRB System, State Banking departments, Department of Agriculture, FDA, the AMA, and others.

Even so called "ghost writers" were trained in the language of political correctness. Many fake studies were written supporting the effectiveness and safety of various products. Experts then are paid quite well to put their names on these fraudulent studies.

A Netherworld of mythical ideas and information had already begun.

Richard continued to experience a great pump for the triceps, which comprise about two thirds of the arm, sometimes adding an inch of growth during a workout session. The close grip barbell version of the bench press worked best for him.

After his last of five sets, he said: "These risks must be managed properly to ensure optimal spiritual and physical well being."

They knew that with each lifting movement for every set strictly performed, the result was not only improved muscularity, but enhanced character, which together carried over to other aspects of life – perseverance and ability to adjust and adapt one's behavior to the ever changing living environment.

Early on, the team recognized that the only constant factor in life is CHANGE.

Richard turned to Johannes who was performing repetitions of barbell curls with respectable poundages, and waited until he was finished.

Then he said: "do you mean that the objective of the USDA is to intentionally <water down> the standards for the farming of organic produce and reasonable animal husbandry in favor of factory farming that uses chemical fertilizers, pesticides, and creates organisms that are modified genetically?"

"The organic label means that the produce in the package is not only safe to eat, but its content does not imperil the environment."

"Also, a rollback of the higher standards for the organic labeling would be replaced with wording such as (according to nature, or nature's best) and country of origin, how the animals are bred

ADRIAN VOGT

and whether the organic produce has been irradiated" would be deleted.

Johannes and Richard became silent when they sorted through the very large credit file.

The file contained extensive recalls of fresh produce, due to unsanitary conditions, and the hysterical calls for the irradiation of most raw foodstuffs to "protect the public."

One prominent U.S. Senator even agreed to allow the major food companies to purchase the portable irradiation equipment to be used in the fields and barns of major factory farmers.

One Senator representing a state in the American "Breadbasket" even uttered such nonsense as: "Ah laak muh beef raer, so ahm fo dat be zapped!"

Alistair couldn't have been more pleased to learn about this most "progressive" development. He ordered a higher number of the portable irradiators to match the rising demand.

That Year, 2007, showed a trend of inferior quality of foodstuffs, the monopolistic factory farmers and food processors continued to ignore the voluntary standards of food safety.

The credit file contained an officer's review of fresh and processed foods labeled as produced by so called conventional methods: the use of pesticides, genetically modified organisms, chemical fertilizers, and other inputs not considered in the organic code of conduct.

Johannes and Richard also remarked to the rest of the team that the management of financial, food and pharmaceutical risks are quite similar.

"Losses in financial and individual health care are due to weak oversight of financial and health conditions, the overall result is the same."

For example, Asian and European banks were the most aggressive buyers of the mortgage backed securities, depending on the evaluations of the rating agencies, instead of their own critical analyses.

The team continued to downgrade asset portfolios if the internal reviews matched those of the rating agencies. Some files contained terse comments; "refer to the analysis by Moodys' or Standard & Poors."

Memoranda of customer credit officers referred to the Basle Committee of Banking Supervision Project II as the Capital Requirements for risk assets rated according to Rating Agency analyses!

The Bank for International Settlements in Switzerland had allegedly given its blessing to this savings of time and cost analysis based on disproportional internal modelling detailing expected default in various tranches of asset secured investments.

If this was true, what did the elitist type of mathematical Geniuses do to compensate for the real losses sustained by all investors in these securities?

The use of the Fear Scenario of the domino effect of failing banks and systemic losses to the average citizen would be used with great aplomb, pomp and circumstance engineered by the clever lobbyists and their malleable political connections.

The result: the huge cash flow of tax revenues could be tapped into!

Other voluminous credit files offering clues to the behavior of the Top Dogs and their Bitches in Big Pharma offered a look into the memoranda of the credit officers.

Those files of the very large participants in the Big Pharma Segment reflected huge profits of new medications, and to stifle claims of negative side effects and mediocre results, huge reserves for legal fees arising from class action lawsuits of alleged harmed patients and doctors were set aside – a cost of doing business!

The files indicated an overriding theme of continued cash flow against to be settled in the future type of lawsuits – a sort of arbitrage, sometimes lasting up to several years. In the meantime, drug company shareholder value continued its meteoric rise!

Johannes thought now of the creature. It had warned him about the Top Dogs and their Bitches at the executive level, they would make the same mistakes, appear self-assured, sometimes behaving in a "blowhard" fashion, and misreading the end consumer's wishes.

"Beautiful! To have our way, we simply tell the Regulators to FUCK OFF!"

They simply wanted their fair share: a 25% Retrurn on Equity!

Wishful thinking! The fools must have their Veil removed from their Faces!"

"End Result: More Glitter than Substance!"

The team was not totally aware that Alistair had already reviewed the same files – behind closed doors, of course.

These files now in stacked order stood about five feet tall in the corner of the MPAG boardroom.

The next day, the team began anew their tedious work to ascertain the true value of risk assets.

One particular file dealt with the pros and cons of using nuclear waste as a raw material for the irradiation of foodstuffs, medical instruments and other areas requiring complete sanitary conditions.

Very controversial would be an understatement for this technology. Scientists and Consumer groups were split in opinion, lawmakers wanted it at the insistence of their lobbyist groups.

After reviewing several more credit officer's memoranda, the team ascertained that, at best, all of these food processing methods did enhance the preservation of edible foods. But at a cost: processing rendered, for example, a steep decline in the assimilation by the body of essential vitamins, minerals, enzymes.

As portrayed in the file, the most avid promoters were the US Government via Departments of Energy, Agriculture, and the Food and Drug Administration (FDA).

Nine years of discussion of the disposal of nuclear waste led to the ideal site for storage of thousands of tons of nuclear waste at the remote Yucca Mountain in Nevada. After an estimated 10,000 years of storage, the deterioration of the containers would only permit a minor amount of leakage in the ground water!

The reviewers of the file would later discover that most of the information about the peace time use of nuclear energy was false – another product of ghost writing!

At his office downtown, Alistair remembered how Secure Systems was started; not long before the destruction of the WTC. Those events hastened the development of the first irradiators.

He was told by his Korean War buddy how potentially profitable the new business would be.

In the year to follow the contracts were easy to obtain because fear was at its highest level – the anthrax scare, food safety, and the Space program provided the necessary impetus for the company to become profitable after only 6 months!

"Awlistaeer," he drawled, "weee cain have awll guvenmen contraxx to irradiate food, aaeend staerillise eenyting aend everryting!"

They also reminisced about tie yuuung aisiann cawwl gurrls.

They chortled: "weeee head awrr faiiir shaeh!"

Alistair suddenly recalled that the file returned to the examination team contained a newspaper clipping about a very controversial murder in Brazil.

He muttered. "Dammit! Who would see that article? Would Johannes see it?"

We have to get that file back and destroy that newspaper clipping!

And, any negative examination results could be altered to our advantage, he mused.

A State of Disarray

That controversial piece was dated May 30, 2008 and appeared next to an article which dealt with the issue of dangerous long lived radioactivity in China. The authorities struggled to make the waste problem less toxic to human and animal life, but with few tangible results.

But Alistair also smiled remembering that the same Wall Street Journal contained an obituary of Dr. Alice Stewart, a renowned British Epidemiologist, who scientifically proved the causality of many cancers with the exposure to various levels of radioactivity over time.

Her findings compelled many scientists and government leaders to reassess their plans for the expansion of the production of uranium and the peace time use of radioactive waste products.

Alistair was pleased to know the death of this person; it paved the way for eliminating delays in the production of the irradiators by Secure Systems.

He also thought about the problem of persistent small operational problems, when taken together might create a HUGE weakness in any operation, whether commercial or financial.

Of course, he did not want to consider further this aspect in examination reports on his desk!

The other very incendiary piece of news in the May 30, 2008 edition, hit very close to home.

Johannes must not see this piece.

He also recalled that Raffy had interrupted his lascivious thoughts about a new intern – coal black hair and curvy. She had creamy coffee-like colored skin and her gait was like a well-bred Mare.

His alter Ego asked: "Would you like to fuck her?"

Shit, he thought. Not now, Raffy!

He would return to THAT subject later.

Alistair knew in advance that at some point in the future it would "pan out"- like finding gold nuggets in the murky water of a mining sluice, to know about Rosa's very wealthy family of ranchers in Brazil.

He read slowly the article, paused frequently between each of the paragraphs.

The Court Process for the murdered Nun and Environmental Activist, Dorothy Stang, was lengthy.

Stang dedicated her life to defending the Brazilian rainforest from depletion from agriculture, illegal logging and ranching.

She worked as an advocate for the rural poor beginning in the early 1970s, helping peasants make a living by farming small plots and extracting forest products without deforestation.

She also sought to protect peasants from criminal gangs working on behalf of ranchers who were after their plots.

One day, she was assassinated by a hit-man hired by several wealthy ranching families.

Alistair paused and read about his wife's wealthy ranching family accused as a co-conspirator in the death of the Nun.

Alistair mused: the Good, the Bad and the Ugly!

He also thought of the negotiation of a large purchase of irradiators with Rosa's very large ranching family.

Secure Systems could reap an enormous profit windfall from the irradiation of select cuts of beef that would be preserved for at least two years in their plastic wrapped form.

Once opened, the smell of fresh butchered meat could be the "clincher" for the consummation of a long term contract – what is there not to like, Alistair thought?

He would soon conclude contracts with Space Administrations globally; after broiling in their space capsule oven, astronauts could enjoy the taste of a filet mignon!

Soldiers in the field could enjoy the moment of a freshly cooked steak in the field!

Johannes read the same piece, and noticed a recent picture of the Family which included two women who resembled twin sisters – Rosa's Mother and Rosa.

The Creature's admonishment came to mind!

He leafed through the file to find more evidence against Alistair and his secret insider trading activities.

He reviewed Examination Reports, which Johannes took before they could go into the schredder.

The reports went back to more than five years, and indicated the presence of internally contrived constraints against any improvement in the control environment of MPAG, New York.

Johannes and his team enjoyed this good, old detective work – one could easily discover the "Bad, and the Ugly" of a sloppy operation; the "Good" was difficult to find, tho.

Preparation is KEY, when one is fighting these battles with an incompetent management.

Nevertheless, there is no substitute for thorough investigative work into the details of an operational function: discussion with the person performing the task, reviewing their daily work, and after-hours processing and booking the transaction.

Such a thorough review could easily determine the adherence or lack thereof, to the established and documented by the management, if any, policy and procedure.

The team realized with each passing day, that the strict practice of "hands on" tried and proven examination procedure is disappearing, in favor of a "One World Order" of technological supervision.

Johannes again reminded the team that they are the Remnant Faithful for "hands on" procedures that are responsible for honest and uncompromising truths.

Johannes spoke to the team about the importance of being prepared for the perilous times to come as Morality takes a backseat to ambitious gain – at all costs.

THIS PICTURE DOESN'T HANG STRAIGHT

They, the Elite and their political minions resist honest, time consuming, and yes, it costs more, to conduct thorough examinations.

After many weeks onsite at the MPAG New York branch, the team concluded that the control environment should be rated as "unsatisfactory" and needs much attention from the management.

Copies of the draft report were presented to Alistair and Fernanda.

They read through the report, pausing between each of the many listed weaknesses and criticisms.

Both of the most senior officers of the New York branch of the venerable Federal Reserve System appeared nervous and moved around frequently in their leather upholstered chairs as they noticed the exceptionally high frequency of irregular operations weaknesses which required the management's immediate resolution!

A real slap in the face! Their client had really screwed the pooch!

Stability in operations was clearly shakey!

If one could view the intestines of Alistair and Fernanda, these organs resembled boiled spaghetti, certainly a feeling of nausea would follow, like an evening of excessive alcohol intake, as they considered the many operations weaknesses.

Perhaps they were sitting on a ticking explosive device, or a huge carbuncle popping its angry red yellow pus in their faces.

Alistair remained speechless, no time now for clever talk, the report must be swept under the carpet, he thought.

If the report was made known to others, in particular, the

Rating Agencies, how would they react to the embarrassing number of potential problems that could impact their computer driven analyses of risk asset default scenarios and portfolio losses?

How would they think in the situation that Alistair and Fernanda found themselves in?

An hour before the meeting with Johannes, they heard the admonishing words of the former head of the Federal Deposit Insurance Corporation (FDIC): "Financial Supervision must be more vigilant, too many things have slipped between the chairs!"

What should that mean?

At least, the former Head doesn't have to worry anymore about the problems of the industry, since he now has become an adviser to the industry; his hands remain clean, perhaps manicured, and wearing fine cufflinks on tailored shirts.

He is free from the political Fray, he does not now risk his reputation on any developing Debacle in the industry. His fighting days are over.

The Report from Johannes and his team could have the effect of an industrial circle saw chewing up the back sides of all of the tenth floor management and it would take many reconstructive surgeries to eventually smooth out their respective Asses.

As was customary, a summary of the examination findings was presented beforehand to the tenth floor management, to make sure that the New York District would not be subjected to embarrassing questions from the media.

Of course, it was up to Alistair and Fernanda to somehow quash this report, was the personal reply of Big Bill, a former Naval Admiral who mastered the romance languages, and impressed so many of the New York bank management scene with his "business smarts."

Big Bill: "Tenemos que de alguna Manera suprimir este Reporte!"

His wife was also a "well connected" Brazilian, and a close friend of Rosa.

They are being haunted by their Sins of Omission: the many Exceptions to real corrective action, which they granted to their client base, may no longer be possible, they thought.

Their "snooty" bank managements would harangue Alistair and Big Bill with comments like: "we feel like pressed lemons, our juice is being siphoned off into a Jar filled with unfiltered seeds, and we don't have the time to remove the seeds to provide drinkable Juice!"

Wow! Damning comments of their own making!

Alistair and Fernanda poured through the report, noting the huge number of operational irregularities.

Internal audit received the most attention. It was the weakest part of the operation.

The team rated the overall control environment as "unacceptable."

Johannes whispered: "The Worst is yet to come."

The two turned to him, and said: "What do you mean by saying that, Johannes?"

ADRIAN VOGT

"That the Head Auditor did almost nothing to document the necessary tasks to review all operations of the branch."

"The Linchpin of any decent management of a bank or a branch rests on the effectiveness of an audit staff to pinpoint weaknesses and have these immediately resolved."

"No pissing around with this or that – action!"

Alistair and Fernanda listened intently to Johannes, as he continued: "The audit department must be completely revamped to reflect at least industry practices:

1. Requesting Documents. ...
2. Preparing an Audit Plan. ...
3. Scheduling an Open Meeting. ...
4. Conducting Fieldwork. ...
5. Drafting a Report. ...
6. Setting Up a Closing Meeting.

"In addition, there was no evidence of risk analyses and rating methods. The most damning part of this examination was the almost complete lack of workpapers demonstrating that even the work was performed!"

The Plan was presented orally to Johannes and his staff. And, after one year, the team discovered that only half of the work was performed.

"Head office in Frankfurt was not even informed of the work plan and results!"

"I did not see that coming," said Alistair, referring to the surprise findings of the compliance review by Simone von Tronchin.

"Of the more than three hundred accounts opened for United

Nations employees, only ten contained sufficient information to identify clearly whether these individuals had sufficient assets to conduct a personal account relationship with the private banking department," said Simone.

She raised her rather bushy eyebrows to make the point that the Know your Customer" guidelines were non-existent, and top management would be hard pressed to determine if any of these persons presented a national security threat to the United States or their home countries!

As with the audit deficiencies, very little about who performed the duties of a compliance officer was formalized in writing!

Outside the board room the muted sound of distant thunder could be heard.

Humidity began to rise not only in the board room but outside as the rain drops began to pound the Park Avenue denizens and unprepared commuters scurrying for cover.

Disarray at a major bank unnerved Johannes. The management should know better.

Alistair's speech of seven years ago to the Group continued to haunt him.

His words were weak, arrogant and unsuitable for examination results in general; that speech to all examiners found little resonance, and created anger and disappointment.

"I am not trying to be an Asshole in such matters, but any sort of changes in important statements about an institution supervised by us or communication with its management must be presented to Fernanda for her final review," stated Alistair.

These words reverberated in his head like a bowling ball striking the Pins in an already very noisy Bowling Alley, as he made up the bed, placing neatly the bed cover over the silky green sheets.

At home with his beautiful Alischraga gave him Solace.

For long moments during the day they held hands, the smooth texture of her rather thick soft fingers communicated healing of his sometimes tortured soul.

Every Saturday he helped her with the house work, he pushed the vacuum cleaner, polished the lacquered rosewood tables and chairs, which they purchased in Hong Kong twenty years ago, planted garden vegetables in huge wooden boxes, and prepared together meals and immediately cleaned up after themselves – they both despised Dissaray.

At that time he recalled the FRBNY's audit department and their delegated responsibility which was very effectively carried out.

He remembered his first job interviews with Alistair, Fernanda, and others of the well experienced staff; they exhibited superior professionalism and real acumen. The FRBNY was way ahead of the other regulatory agencies, in terms of providing outstanding guidance to the supervised banks. At that time they were not viewed as "clients."

That time was more than twenty years ago!

Johannes wondered how the deterioration in attitude and performance could have been so drastically weakened.

Johannes knew the danger of a sick Bureaucracy, run by non-elected officials, similar to a mealy apple whose insides gradually lose flavor and disintegrate into a dried up mess.

The dried up mess amounted to billions of Dollars of property value writeoffs in the real estate mortgage business!

What happened?

Was it the ultimate result of negligent internal control throughout the industry?

Helicopter Ben, the successor Oracle, lamented and gestured wildly about the lack of the necessary tools in the FRB regulatory tool box: "if only we had these tools to prevent this crisis!"

"Of course, Big Bill undertook the responsibility to convey the right answer to the public," said Alistair.

He added: "as a group, we must respect and support the rationale of Big Bill's explanation."

Alistair and Fernanda were no dumb Dogs that would only be content with a few bones thrown in their direction. They needed MEAT to chew on!

They were clever enough to realize that the replacement of the Glass-Steagall Act with the GLB of 1999 was a tragic mistake for the global economy!

They also recognized that during the 1930's the separation of Wall Street trading activities from commercial banking could have prevented the 2008-2009 Crisis, if left intact.

Of course, it was self-evident to Johannes and the team that the strict observance to adequate credit review standards would have at least reduced the severity of the Sub-Prime Crisis.

It was difficult to watch how this Crisis resembled the HIV

ADRIAN VOGT

Pandemic that swept across the Globe and caused substantial damage to all countries' economies.

Exactly like the unelected officials of regulatory agencies charged with the responsibility to protect the public from substandard conditions in the Big Pharma and Agricultural sectors.

The lack of enforcement is now endemic, even the political environment resonated with hesitation and uncertainty.

But the question still lingered in Johannes' Mind: "Who would undertake the responsibility to enforce the supervisory recommendations contained in the MPAG report?"

Johannes could push through the relentless followup actions needed to repair any operational weaknesses at any major bank that could cause a potential crisis in the financial markets.

All he needed was the Blessing of Alistair, Fernanda, and Big Bill.

And, this could be possible, he reasoned, because he enjoyed an excellent reputation within the System of Reserve Banks.

He and his team showed no fear of any top management at the largest banks and investment firms. What could be the principal reason for this courageous attitude?

He and his team knew how and when to ask the "right questions, and these always focused on basic principles of credit approval and repayment and operational integrity.

And, Alistair liked his style.

Johannes enjoyed listening to the whining voices of the bank managements.

204

He could overhear their panic-stricken voices as they called Alistair to exert pressure against the team's controversial findings.

Even the team questioned the external auditors' opinions on the appropriate matching of revenue and expense that could lead to reversal of short term trading profits and losses.

How dare they counter the external auditors' opinions!

Such a direction in favor of conservative accounting principles could reduce projected earnings per share and the perceived reduction in shareholder value only exacerbated their screams for relief!

They hated him and his team. There was no professional courtesy extended to THESE EXAMINERS.

Why? Self-explanatory, the team was just too good.

The older and more experienced examiners of the FRBNY that remained close friends of Alistair performed excellent training for Johannes and his team.

Those days of the 1980's were long gone – the newer staff could not adjust to the hard work of true auditing and hours-long reviews of risk assets to determine true liquidating value, if required, outside of borrower cash flow, would be needed to repay on time or at maturity its contractual debt.

During a telephone conversation with Alistair he learned of another attempt by Congress to consolidate all regulatory agencies to avoid another major crisis.

Alistair: "the discussion revealed reluctance on the part of Representative Franks and Senator Dodd that a certain value still exists with the present overlapping regulatory systems."

ADRIAN VOGT

Alsitair compared the current embarrassing situtation with the muscular size of a bodyguard hired by a group of well made up female singers who showed to advantage their physical attributes to their worshipping public. It was important to demonstrate their Security detail!

"The same with us, a symbolic gesture, and the intention behind the Charade was always rather disgusting!"

"Johannes, did you really think this Situation resembled the beautiful muscular back side of a beeeeoooootifuuull woman?"

"Or should we always observe the front side?"

"Which is more rapturous, Johannes?"

As Alistair laughed lustily, he showed the entire array of his white teeth, seemingly without cavities.

"These Washington DC assholes do not earn their Keep!"

"Politically, I don't believe they would really do anything to uphold the laws of the land; I mean the U.S. Constitution."

"They orient themselves to their own Enrichment, they revel in their unlimited access to taxpayer funds, spending money that doesn't belong to them."

"They think we're foolish pieces of Shit."

"Irredeemable."

In the back of Alistair's mind, was the threat of arbitration between MPAG management and the Board of Governors!

Egg on the faces of Alistair and Fernanda was a distinct

206

possibility, if they had to defend the team's findings in front of the Oracle and the other Governors, as the new risk focused procedures did not protect their clients from the onslaught of Johannes' very thorough review.

Johannes and his team did not follow the new "Rules of the Road."

It might show that they had lost control over their own staff!

Was this an open rebellion?

Was this a modern day Mutiny on the Bounty?

Alistair and Fernanda were caught in a vice – on the one hand, they sympathized with the team, on the other side, their commitment to a kinder and gentler supervision ethic, would ensure their career at the New York District.

Alistair thought of his fine lifestyle with Rosa and their social position among the important personalities of New York City; she would not take kindly to any potential diminution of reputation and prestige.

Any banking controversy in the New York Times mentioning her "Alistair" as a responsible regulator for a foreign institution undergoing severe operational problems must be quashed, she thought.

There had already been precedent: a major foreign bank reported huge trading losses as a result of weak operational controls and faulty head office supervision. That was in 1995, ten years ago.

How could this be done without much Fanfare?

She had to protect her luxurious lifestyle and HER ALISTAIR.

That evening she discussed the situation with her man. He showed her a copy of the examination results summary. She gasped at the long list of criticisms that were the center piece of the findings.

Her long career at that Brazilian bank with her German boyfriend enabled her to realize how serious the operational weaknesses were.

After several minutes of long discussion, they had the solution.

They would go after the team.

And not in a pleasant way!

Prelude to Survival

Although the planned elimination of the team appeared fail safe, Alistair and Rosa had not calculated all risks of failure in their scheme.

Chief among the potential risk of failure was one person – Miguelito Pohlmann, a relatively recent arrival from the communist country of Cuba.

While still in Cuba he took notes in class about military history, often colored with the propaganda against the American interventionists in Latin American affairs.

However, on one of his several visits to Havana, he walked in a back alley off the main drag – "black market" book store that offered American military history books, including the Civil War.

Miguelito leafed through the partially yellowed pages in a book about civil war military heroes.

He remembered that quote of the best known General of the Civil War: "War is War and it is not a popular Competition."

William Tecumseh Sherman was one of Miguelito's favorite military heroes. An avid reader of American History, he wanted to be certain that he could learn something from these famous people.

After arriving in the Miami, Florida area, he took on odd jobs to earn enough money to purchase firearms and ammunition. He immediately became a member of the National Rifle Association.

His prior life in communist Cuba was not easy: Communism decreed that God did not exist. Church buildings were occupied by the military. Bibles, if found, were destroyed.

The new government confiscated all private property, everything is now owned by the Castro regime. A vast difference in Communist Ideology: the Italians allowed private property, the Maoists – none, everything turned over to the State.

His father, Uwe, was a prominent East German engineer that had already designed and built a number of important infrastructure projects.

His Mother, Erika, a very beautiful Cuban –provided to the Regime gourmet type meals from their very adequate kitchen; the family after the Castro revolution was moved to a villa outside of Havana, once owned, so the rumor goes, by a family with close ties with the American Central Intelligence Agency (CIA).

As there were always exceptions to the new Dogma, the Pohlmanns lived better than most. Uwe Pohlmann enjoyed a certain prestige in the German Democratic Republic, even close ties with the female head of the East German Secret Service.

The former owners, also rumored to be in prison, suffered unimaginable physical and mental torture at the hands of the revolutionaries. Male and female political prisoners endured continued harassment at the hands of the perverted.

Miguelito grew up in Los Palacios in Pinar del Rio, a

northwestern province of Cuba. The tropical climate throughout the year even provided cool evenings for wearing light jackets.

Most of the family income came from rice farming and retail grocery operations on a small scale.

Uwe made good money from his construction business for the East German and Castro governments. East German Marks were equivalent to the hard currency West German Deutschemark – artificially supported via transfer payments from the western zone to the eastern zone.

It wasn't long, however, before the Pohlmanns were viewed as outsiders by the locals.

The Communist "Upper Crust" became less popular after the Revolution, when all private property was confiscated except theirs!

The government owned everything now!

Only the Communist Party members and their families had enough hard currency to shop at the "Hard Currency" stores – jewelry, fine clothing, fresh produce, etc.

The Communist Manifesto was now nothing more than another dictatorship, replacing the corrupt Regime of Fulgencio Batista.

The block captains and their Snitches were rewarded if they were able to find something on someone being "disloyal" to the Regime.

Something, anything!

The decision for the Pohlmanns to leave was easy; but only

the son was allowed to leave, since the parents were viewed as too important to the Success of the Revolution!

The East German government also needed the Pohlmanns to remain in Cuba to maintain its influence in Latin America, and further develop the military infrastructure.

Uwe was distantly related to the Scientist Werner von Braun, who developed the first missiles aimed at the british mainland, the buzz bombs and the V-2 Rockets.

Miguelito was not quite fifteen years old when his parents convinced him that he had to leave first, or he would be drafted into mandatory service. Then they would somehow follow.

He only had his "Gusano", a five foot long duffel bag made out of coffee sack material, it resembled a long worm. It contained a tooth brush, sandals, two pairs of underwear, and necessary identity Documents showing he actually was compelled to leave Cuba by the Communist government.

Relatives that were on the same flight were not frightened. They left a worse kind of fear: prior to leaving they were stripped naked by the well armed guards to see if they were carrying anything of value, even cavity searches on the better looking women were conducted.

The last moment prior to leaving Cuba, he was gripped with fear, but Erika told him: "You will find work somewhere, mechanics are needed everywhere."

Autos were his specialty – particularly the fast ones!

During the short flight from Havana to Miami via "Cubana de Aviacion", he assured himself again and again that he was a "damned good" mechanic.

His mother told him: "Remember, Miguelito, we are here to work, not lay around and take welfare!"

Some years later, Miguelito still had these words reverberate in his head.

The start was loud and uneven, as the twin engines belched black smoke, probably because of the plane sitting on the tarmac for at least 24 hours.

The rising humidity almost flooded the two motors.

The much older model Sikorsky during the trip shook violently in response to the frequent "air pockets", which served to generate passengers' prayers and crying of an imminent crash in the ocean, that their very familiar life in Paradise was lost forever, did not enter their minds.

When he observed closely the airstrip concrete, on the near perfect landing of this "puddle jumper", he realized almost immediately that his new life turned positive, although he did not know why.

The plane's engines became silent, and all fifty passengers disembarked, he was the last one off the plane. Suddenly, a new fear came upon him. Who would pick him up at the Miami Airport?

Relatives unknown to him appeared at the Exit, carrying a sign – Miguelito Pohlmann – introduced themselves to him, and he felt relieved!

And, at the curb of the Arrivals section, he saw a brand new Buick Skylark with other relatives sitting and waiting for the new arrival!

Some years later his parents escaped on a plane piloted by a well known General on Castro's staff, avoiding anti-aircraft fire at dusk was their only cover: it worked!

Uwe operated a service station in Miami located on Calle Ocho.

Erika took odd jobs as a housekeeper, until her gourmet chef skills were discovered by the home owners.

Their first home was located in a lower income area of Miami, Florida. After several years, the Marielitos arrived, and decent housing became scarce. The area of Hiahleah became more popular with those that had not yet mastered the English language. From a very "rundown" area to one offering potential became the rallying cry for all exiled Cubans! Hard work and the opportunity to improve one's economic circumstances became a poster child of a true representation of Capitalism!!

The fruits of hard work and a capitalistic society reaped huge dividends for the Pohlmanns. They wisely invested in real estate in poorer areas of the City, previously occupied by other minority groups who subsequently moved to other suburbs of the Greater Metropolitan Mami.

Relatives choosing to stay behind in communist Cuba did not fare as well.

The Pohlmanns soon forgot the difficulties they faced in leaving their Homeland, since their improved prosperity was a direct result of an economic system allowing private ownership.

Also, they enjoyed the fruits of their labor as immigrants arriving legally, as proud Cubans they strictly followed all immigration laws.

Soon after arriving in Miami, Miguelito became a staunch

THIS PICTURE DOESN'T HANG STRAIGHT

supporter of gun rights, he made certain that he was able to purchase an arsenal of weapons to defend himself, his family, and his closest friends – Alischraga Saleh and Johannes Emmerich.

They had befriended him when he first arrived in Miami, Florida, and helped him find work.

He soon recognized that the color of his skin was not fair – rather a cinnamon hue was evident.

He could be mistaken for a black man. However, his black colleagues all agreed that the possession of guns kept them safe rather than being unarmed.

In 1964 the Deacons for Defense and Justice, an armed African-American group was founded to protect civil rights activists and their families. During the Civil War black men used guns to fight for their freedom.

Also, Miguelito knew that the time was coming when people will not endure sound teaching, many will turn away from listening to the truth and wander into myths.

Mythical ideas that Christianity only served to enrich white people were not totally accepted by the new arrivals since they escaped the atheistic dogma of Fidel Castro and his strict acceptance of Maoist communism.

To protect his hard won Freedom, he knew that he had to fight all forms of Despotism.

He soon recognized that he would not spend much time on watching and listening to the negative news being broadcast.

Miguelito mentiond to his parents: "The major media is filled

215

ADRIAN VOGT

with reports about all the bad things people are doing and the evil running rampant in the world."

Satan must be behind all the negative newscasters, he thought. For answers, he relied on God's grace and the historical negativity that can impact a country greatly.

The Civil War was one of those negative events perpetuated by the Confederate slave owners.

So much Suffering, he muttered.

He began to realize that his role in his new homeland was to do the work of an Evangelist, so to speak, to fulfil his own God-given Destiny.

Like so many legal immigrants that arrived before the Pohlmanns, the drawing card to America was religious freedom.

Fidel Castro had allowed the once impressive structures dominated by the powerful Catholic Church to fall to the whims of pigeons, defecating in the rafters and marble floors of the now empty buildings.

The powerful Roman Catholic Church offered not even a whimper of resistance against the Communist Regime.

He also recognized that the immigration to that land only 90 miles away had really become a farce.

But not because of Cuban immigrants, since they followed the rules.

It was that other ilk of immigrant that kowtowed to the whims of the elitist Masquerade of unlimited benefits for all – take other

216

people's hard earned social security and health insurance through falsified documents and other unsavory means.

He soon heard how and why those elitist bastards promoted the idea that everyone in the world can come to America.

The major players cooperated with the other countries wanting to get rid of their over populated problems, even printing broschures to show the "ins and outs" of skirting the immigration laws.

Even the American advertising lobbyists ran ads depicting stupid old men from all parts of the world who could hardly speak a word of English, and stuttering: "Ahh, emmm een Ehmericun !"

They tried to say: "I am an American!"

The peak of this advertising stupidity occurred in the 1990's, when the diminished middle classs began to protest the continued job loss to cheap labor countries, only to be replaced by those jumping the fence going straight to the head of the line, so to speak.

One day, he mused, his arsenal would become even more pivotal for the elimination of political and elitist disequilibrium to restore the middle class – the dregs of society, according to some politicians.

He had heard that type of divisive language before.

He would do his part to differentiate the truth from the falsehoods and lies of Satan – represented by his messengers of confusion in Washington D.C. that continued to blow smoke up the asses of Los Estupidos!

To attend the University was not a big part of his future plans, instead he wanted to operate his own business.

His female companion of three years – a strong looking Cuban woman with wonderful physical Attributes - built for the rack, he thought many times, however, not only physically satisfying, but a superb business person – she had a wonderful acumen for investment timing and when to pull back from the brink.

She was not afraid of risk taking. Within the three years with her, they had accumulated a net worth of more than six figures. Quite simple, she told others: "the Communists could not take away what was already in her head!"

He not only managed a successful auto mechanic business, but his formerly imprisoned relatives in Cuba finally left with the Marielitos and opened a small weapons manufacturing business.

Their still broken English stated aggressively: "Nooow, nobaddy wa gonna monkey aroun with uuuss!"

They produced bullet proof glass, bullet proof vests, copied several varieties of Glock and Sig Sauer pistols. Bullet production was easy for them – they really demonstrated a much needed skill in the Miami area.

Heavy weaponry was also provided to the police force in Miami – in particular, machine guns and Gatlin hardware.

Of course, only available to the local SWAT team – not totally known to the Dade County Commissioners.

"Do whatever you have to do to keep order!" Such statements were kept under wraps.

After a few years Johannes caught up with Miguelito and further bolstered their already strong affinity for each other.

Johannes said jokingly, that he could diversify his activities by opening a Limo service to drive the Rich and Famous around, and deposit their monies in legitimate offshore accounts.

"What are you trying to do ? Kill me!?"

Yaaahhh, Haaah, Hah!!

Since those three years, Miguelito grew even more in height: now 6 foot 4", lifting Olympic weights approaching world records!

Perhaps in the tradition of the Cuban weightlifters of OLD, always dominating the Pan American Games every summer during the 1950s, thought Johannes.

Even almost qualifying for the Olympics in 2000, but a knee injury sustained in a motorcycle accident while testing the Model of the Indian Brand soon to come back into production, dashed his hopes.

Un Peo en El Cartucho!

Always moving – hard to hit a moving target, mused Johannes over his very loyal friend.

His thoughts now turned to escape and survival.

On this late Autumn evening the moon hung low in the sky, in the forefront of a shadowy Frontier. His hiding place was secure, where Fox and Rabbit would say "Goodnight" to one another.

Near the state of Georgia border, a rustic three-hundred year-old farmhouse still stood large, far from the lights of the big City. It was no Shack. Heavy black colored rocks and stones, like those of a graveyard adorned the outside of the house, a symbol of a solid past life, that all viewing the structure be a witness to a stable time period in American history.

Johannes Emmerich compared it to a new construction, which lacked substance: the new ones were cold and empty in feeling, like the souls of the Lost, who govern this remarkable country, but yet accomplish little of true value.

Solid wood and stone became a rarity, replaced by pressed particleboard with plastic overlay indicating an expensive wood grain and color. Ersatz plastic pieces resembling rock and stone could be recognized.

On the ground lay acorns and beechnuts – a true sign of Fall weather and a deepening weather temperature contrast, that led to more and more Ground Cover, which provided to the wild swine roaming the forests a considerable supply of food.

Also the neighboring corn fields across the road led to several auto accidents during the harvesting as the wild pigs crossed the streets to reach the bountiful clumps of chaff and corn silk residue.

Johannes knew that it was a matter of time before the enemy came for him and his team. The team – the Remnant Faithful - had long split up and went their separate ways and "off the grid."

He could hold off the Band of Killers for a short time. They drove armored vehicles, carried the latest weaponry, and were battle seasoned.

Johannes had two pump action shotguns and two sharp combat knives. But he had the advantage of terrain, and the element of surprise.

They would not expect a thrown knife aimed for the throat, or the sudden presence of grizzly bears.

The shotguns functioned quite well. More reliable than the

semi-automatic ones which on occasion could overheat and the spent shells could be stuck in the barrel.

If this breakdown in functionality were to occur, the presence of a large brown colored Grizzly charging toward the shooter might not work out positively for that person, since one blow to the head from the Bear's giant paw could be "all she wrote" for him.

The bear was not dumb when it came to culinary delights in the forest. It would drag the still warm corpse to a safe hiding place so that other Carnivores would'nt cash in on a new found Freebie! After the body mellowed out a bit, then culinary Joy would begin.

Johannes thoughts dwelled on the events of the prior day.

He cursed that day.

Alistair and Fernanda cautioned Johannes and the team about the Confidentiality of the Examination findings of MPAG New York.

He did not figure that they would all along find some way to prevent the findings to be made known to the Board in D.C.

Alistair and Fernanda made no secret about the sensitive criticisms in the report. If found out: "it would be catastrophic for the industry!'

Fernanda's face turned red as she screamed at him:"you placed no value on the new guidelines – the Rules of the Road!"

"This Report did not adhere to the form and content value for our Client!"

"You and your team have not poined out to the bank "the challenges" they face for the future!"

Fernanda brusquely stated: "Simone, Richard, Bill, Jennifer, Susan, get out of the office now, we want to discuss with your Examiner-in-Charge the rest of the findings!"

The team left quickly and began to disperse, they knew what was coming down the pike.

After the others left their spacious offices, Alistair and Fernanda changed their body language to that of a wild cat before its prey.

"Johannes, do you consider yourself to be a team player?"

"For what reason have you not followed the new Guidelines?"

The interrogation lasted four hours. They tried to have him knuckle under. To no avail.

Johannes decided at the moment not to call them out for their well known transgressons against the insider trading rules of the Board of Governors.

He balled up his fists, armed mentally with the knowledge of Ephesians 5: 5-10 and Collosians 1:10, stood up from his leather upholstered chair, turned his face direct at them, and walked slowly shouting at them as he approached them both.

"For the sake of clarity, his voice was loud and slow: Your cheating and lies will not be observed by me and my team!"

"It is not what you and your friends with the CFF want, the truth is that God's words tell me what to do."

"Our view of the rotten operational environment is Gospel: It is not what the junk of the world wants us to do!"

"The mainstay of our work is the Truth, quitting is not an option for us – we are Soldiers in the Army of the Lord!"

"What the Hell? You embarassed me before my colleagues!"

"Have you no courtesy?"

"Remember, God is watching!"

"When you stand before God, what will you say, when the accounting for your actions is due?"

Alistair and Fernanda were breathless and frozen with fear. They hadn't expected this type of reaction.

"And don't tell me that you don't have enough factual information to throw the book at them!"

"And, we carefully spelled out the corrective actions needed, in our presentation!"

"Also, some of the violations pertaining to the maintenance of accurately calculated capital could result in monetary penalties of US $25 million!"

"And you are going to raise objections to our very thorough examination because of non adherence to report writing rules?"

"You have the nerve to refer to the supervised institutions as clients?"

"Do not be overly prescriptive?"

"What the fuck does that mean?"

A deeper red color appeared on the faces of the Inquisitors, both devout Catholics they are, or at least so they said.

They feared that Johannes' report could cause them to lose their cushy jobs, or worst yet, cause a near collapse of the New York branch of MPAG!

The spectre of disclosure of their numerous insider trading deals would wreak even more trouble on them.

Johannes said: "You are all pieces of Shit!"

"I will stamp you out with my foot! You are aware of what happens to stomped out shit; it dries up and the wind carries the dust globally!"

"That's what happened with the 2008/2009 Real Estate Debacle when the operational weaknesses of the CLIENTS were swept under the Rug!"

Johannes looked menacingly at Alistair and stepped closer to him, opened his clenched fist, his thick long fingers grabbed him by the left shoulder, spun him around, and said:

"You should be fired, you have totally neglected the principles of well known practices to protect depositors from the machinations of Charlatans!"

"I should kick your fucking Ass out of this office, and throw you down the concrete stairs!"

"Then you wouldn't be in any condition to protect your buddies from their transgressions in operations and compliance activities."

"I will not let you destroy these examination reports, you sorry fuck, like those in the 23rd floor paper shredder, in Building Seven of the WTC collapse, estimated to be over eight thousand files of the SEC related to suspicious activities of banks and hedge funds!"

In Effect, .. He hesitated, and glanced at Fernanda.

Her face was pale from fright. She saw Johannes continue to drag Alistair over the soft carpet, then Johannes left him on the floor, stood firmly on both feet, muttered under his breath:"fucking Asshole," then left the office.

During this altercation, Fernanada thought if Johannes had incapacitated Alistair, she could continue her liaison with Rosa, unhampered by guilt.

Among certain members of the Bank Supervision Group she enjoyed a rather controversial reputation. And, why not, she thought, we live in a very tolerant and free society.

She dreamed of previous sultry encounters between her and Rosa: they paraded themselves in a Park Plaza hotel room, wearing only thin negligees, their thick hairy vaginal bushes moving with each sensuous step toward each other to softly embrace one another, then rubbing each of their erect breast nipples vigorously.

Fernanda enjoyed their long kisses, tongueing slowly each corner of their very broad mouths. And, then some.

Fernanda broke every rule of human decency – good that she and Rosa did not live during the time of the Old Testament – they would have been stoned to death – Leviticus Chapters 19 and 20.

Alistair would not fare much better.

Alistair picked himself up off the soft carpet and muttered: "There is no turning back!"

ADRIAN VOGT

The decision to destroy all of the report findings and the entire team was conceived on the evening of a Grand fundraising Gala in the City of Brotherly Love.

The Evening of this Ball focused on the American Heart Association efforts to further educate the public on the dangers of non recognition of potential circulatory problems and their rectification.

The Marriott Hotel featured this Event. Rosa looked her best in a black evening dress that displayed her very fine physical attributes to the fullest.

There were other full busomed women who showed their lifted Big Tits, some with Silicone implanted breasts, quite obvious to the observer, since they did not move with the body.

The Event also honored the new president of the Children's Hospital of Philadelphia.

Alistair was also there to enjoy the Eye Candy.

The location on the Avenue of the Arts in the trendy part of the City provided the Venue for a Victoria's Secret type of display of the finest female clothing, women of all shapes and sizes could pride themselves with their latest wardrobes.

Her man wrote out a very generous check of $10,000, and why not, a pittance against almost daily insider trading profit of ten times that amount.

Always on the prowl for an opportunity in real estate, Alistair and Rosa on the day after the Gala, strolled the area and observed several high rise projects for the wealthy and discriminating younger generation of yuppies who worked tirelessly in their jobs – the rule of thumb for these elitist guys and gals, 16 hour days.

226

If I remember right, this city has a history of ups and downs –
high crime, homeless, corruption in high places, etc.," said Alistair
softly and sensibly to Rosa.

Rosa remained silent. Her man was right.

The historical infrastructure as well as the adminstration
building with the Statue of William Penn standing on its highest
point needed serious renovation.

Splotches of white pigeon Droppings covered much of the
walkways through the area of the city government offices to the
other side of Market Street where the posh retailers, at least those
that had not moved to the Suburbs, operated.

The staircases down to the underground transportation and
walking areas smelled of strong urine, the homeless pissed there
all the time, sometimes, one could smell a hint of cheap wine or
liquor – perhaps Thunderbird or Southern Comfort", the numerous
old, filthy wool blankets to sleep on and the makeshift pillows of old
rags and dingy newspapers, were in plain view of the commuters
and people escaping the brutal winter cold.

And, not unnoticed by the handsome pair, was the onerous
City Wage Tax, which periodically was adjusted upward, seldom
reduced.

With these observations still fresh in their heads, they politely
declined the discounted offers of the Center City real estate brokers.

Other parts of the greater Philadelphia Metropolitan
area indicated too much poverty, murders, welfare recipients
outnumbering even the low wage earner, and terrible winter
weather!

Of positive note was the well maintained Independence

Hall – the Birthplace of the Nation, the Liberty Bell, and other historical points of interest.

After making their decision to hold off on a purchase of a Piece of the City of Brotherly Love, they climbed into their stretch Hummer armor plated Limo chauffeured by one of their favorite male drivers, who incidentally was quite famous in his own right, a member of the Las Vegas, Nevada Troupe – ,"Wonder Down Under," an Australian and Irish male combo of beautiful virile males.

The truth is that Rosa and Alistair counted as one of the Dream Couples of America. Whether in Nice or Davos, as well as other trendy spots of the world, they were socially sought after couples.

They were in the company of some of the most powerful people, including those of the communist world.

Alistair concluded various business transactions during a game of Golf in Davos, while Rosa was busy entertaining other like women in the art of passionate sexual encounters.

Whether on the red carpet in Berlin, Hollywood or Nice, they conducted themselves outwardly as a in Unison" well dressed couple. Alistair wore a conservative Tuxedo with charcoal gray striped pants, Rosa dressed to show just enough skin to excite men and women.

The day after the Fund Raising Gala, the three men and three women assassins had already positioned themselves to carry out their objective.

Rosa did her homework, the Group was only loyal to any governing body, that would pay them their fair share of the to be aquired Booty, as their definition of the word was more akin to what pirates of old could get, of course, they could also adjust to the more modern definition – a beautiful set of Nalgas on a sensuous woman.

The Group was not dumb, they saw the steady deterioration of the middle class in America, and the attendant greed of the CFF in their operations in lands that rapidly lose their moral compass; lands once having substance of character -now only showing more Glitter than on an outrageous plastic Barbie Doll.

Their reputation preceded them for their ability to adjust to a legal system that provides them the right to a fair trial that assumes their innocence until proven guilty, not the other way around – guilty until proven innocent!

Allegedly, the amount paid to them for finding that particular Iraqi Dictator was US$ 25 million! Not exactly chump change.

However, they did not know the exact location in the Hinterland near the City of Brotherly Love where they might encounter Johannes Emmerich.

Upon successful completion of their Mission, they would each receive their share of the Hush Money which amounted to US$One million, for work that should take only a short period of time to complete.

They were really contract killers – the three men and three women – beautiful specimens of humanity, thought Rosa.

Although their respective upbringing in Camden, New Jersey and Philadelphia, Pennsylvania exhibited instability, they persisted in their desire to achieve monetary success at any cost.

And, why not?

They observed that in America, there were many examples of individuals that made it happen - like that Coffee Entrepreneuer, or the many nerdy-looking Computer Geniuses.

They despised those rabble rousing Asshole politicians seeking to further bolster their reputation as Haters of Capitalism and GUNS.

With a Blink of the Eye, they would eliminate the up and coming Diarrhea of the Mouth, espousers of the Wonders of Che Guevara, Fidel Castro, Mao, Vladimir Lenin, Joseph Stalin, Marx and Engels, etc.; in effect taking other people's money for themselves.

They loved the political arena of America – future work for them! With each utterance of a self-serving politician, they added to their stockpile of weaponry and ammo.

Curiously enough, they were staunch supporters of everything about American History – in particular, they enjoyed knowing about the tumulteous military history.

They did not realize how much they had in common with one Miguelito Pohlmann, whom they would soon meet, under difficult circumstances!

They also could not understand the drift away from Patriotism, the defense of the Nation against her enemies, including those of the cowardly Antifa, wearing masks to cover their faces as they paraded placards: More dead cops.

The Group vowed not to stand by while these leftist thugs destroyed the country and attacked innocent citizens.

This cowardly tactic reminded the Group of the Systems of Bolshevism, National Socialism, all of their brothers and sisters committed heinous crimes in the name of justice and equality.

THIS PICTURE DOESN'T HANG STRAIGHT

They wanted to puke when they heard the cowardly, anti-American, greedy politicians, Hollywood actors and radicals voice their vulgar protests against the 22,000 law enforcement officers.

Character assassinations of the voting public who supported the Executive Branch's patriotic actions and defending human decency, were called dregs of society, and deplorables!

Even certain patriotic songs were jeered at: When Johnny Comes Marching Home, and the Battle Hymn of the Republic – songs depicting the return of friends and relatives who were fighting wars for the country.

They were brave veterans, who sacrificed themselves for their country, they would suffer more and more inasmuch as they still belonged to that group of disabled, yet battle ready individuals anxious to make a difference.

What did that really mean? Make a difference in what?

Did they really think things through when they would sign up again and again for more active duty in exotic places?

It doesn't matter any more since their disabilities centered in the post traumatic stress syndrome (PTSD) condition, most of the veterans still had some issues after a brief period of Rehab state side.

The PTSD emanated from powerful bomb explosions, which created immense shock waves, strong enough to throw one to the ground, or against building walls, which were in the immediate vicinity.

According to military experts, the exposure to the sudden impact of the explosion pressure led to damage in the central nervous system, headaches, and erratic thought processes.

Was it really worth the investment in brave and patriotic soldiers to invade Iraq and Afghanistan?

These thoughts were bandied about by the six veterans.

Or would they now work for private contractors? Similar to the Brackwater LLC? Or through wealthy individuals?

The maladies of war were carried each day by these good-looking soldiers of fortune. Now known as Rosa's Army, they had to write on paper almost every thought emanating in their head!

The PTSD condition enabled them to mentally processs only ideas of a short term nature; long term – forget it!

But, no matter. They loved America!

But for the wrong reasons: the Authorities and their extensive laws and regulations, in many cases, were not fully adhered to.

In general, this Group of PTSD veterans quickly caught on to the lack of real enforcement in the broad system of Regulation conditioned by the lack of competent individuals – laws were made by men, they mused.

Their readiness to take on projects involving hard work did not go unnoticed by the CFF and Rosa.

Their reputation for performing the tunnel work under the American-Mexican Border became well-known, and their work offered them the chance to enter into other interesting highly remunerative lines of work.

The political connections of Alistair and Rosa kept the law enforcement at bay, as interesting sources of cash flow" for the cooperating officials were always available.

THIS PICTURE DOESN'T HANG STRAIGHT

Skilled specialized labor became their forte: the removal of 30 kilo heavy manhole covers at any hour of the evening and early morning hours to accommodate certain underworld projects brought in more and more cash.

The manhole covers were easily carried by each one of them, since a part of their daily physical training entailed the walking exercise of carrying 45 pound olympic barbell plates in each hand for rather long distances – the so called Farmer's Walk exercise.

The Group was considered an outsider in the system, however, they did not view themselves as illegals, taking advantage of the generous american taxpayer.

They were aware of the greedy powerful lobbyists, multis, Big Pharma, factory farmers, and the other parasitic freeloaders, having no conscience ripping off the American taxpayer.

Also, reliance on government assistance would leave a paper trail, Rosa and Alistair wanted no undesirable attention drawn to their rather controversial extra curricular activities!

In this case, less is bettter.

Other endeavors of the group included U.S. Mexico Border patrols in relatively secluded areas where the Drug Cartels and the smuggling of alleged terrorsts from Yemen, Bangladesh, and other countries occur.

These system outsiders quietly conducted their clean up operations along the porous border; the media never covered these incidents – numerous bodies of alleged terrorists scattered throughout the remote rural areas of Texas, Arizona are never found in one location.

The group is extremely mobile and blends in well in the particular environment known for illicit activity.

Sort of like Chamelions, removable tatoos, face mask disguises, images of deadbeats, conservative dressers, etc., whatever the environment calls for, is their Modus Operandi.

The question is why would these six individuals hired by Rosa behave in this manner?

They love the opportunities for employment and profit in promising situations – America, land of the free, home of the brave, offers the best work for them – after all is said and done, they want to protect the Beacon of Hope for all – not destroy it, as Satan and its Minions want to do.

The Battle of Good versus Evil? Well, not quite.

Their personal backgrounds in the greater Camden, New Jersey and Philadelphia, Pennsylvania metropolitan areas centered on- yes, you guessed it – frequent activities with the opposite sex.

The Group had expensive tastes- they enjoyed La Vida Loca. They could, because they believed that it was good to be them."

They were very good-looking specimens – brown almost mahogany colored skin, black hair, muscular, and young enough still to be conspicuous.

No surprise that Rosa wanted this group, when accompanying her they could fit in with her good looks.

The Group's arrogance was not ill-founded. They grew up in the same neighborhood as Rosa in Brasilia, the Capitol City.

At the University, they knew Rosa and became good friends, so much so, that anyone looking at her in a disrespectful way, would receive an avalanche of kicks and punches.

With this tough guy reputation, they would not receive their certificate of higher learning.

And, unknown to their many friends of both sexes, they provided Protection to the early developing Rappers – they enjoyed the extreme, and sometimes violent Text of their brand of music, delivered illegal drugs, and weapons.

When immigrating to America, they settled in the City of Brotherly Love and Camden, the global Headquarters of Campbell Soup.

Their living on the edge activities centered in the "Philadelphia Badlands", a section of North Philadelphia, Pennsylvania, United States, that is known for an abundance of open-air recreational drug markets and drug-related violence.

They soon moved out of this area, for a variety of reasons, the remaining decent behaving neighbors ignored them, the Group became tired of the unreliable garbage pickup service, rotting garbage and the shit smeared baby diapers laying on the concrete steps to the subway, sometimes mixed with empty fast food containers, spilling out of plastic bags too small to use.

While these socially disadvantaged" still received their welfare checks, even the social workers stayed away!

The Group wanted to be far away from this Misery.

It wasn't always this bad, said a few remaining neighbors, that still had jobs.

Fifty years ago, the area was a manufacturing district for major corporations, neighborhoods were clean and well maintained, a strong middle class contingent was the rule not the exception.

But the concept of outsourcing" came in to vogue; move the jobs to low wage countries, and the displaced middle class worker was offered adjustment assistance (AA) and re-training to learn new skills.

In theory, this idea of AA made some sense; however, reality took hold and the CFF made certain this idea would not gain traction.

The Unions and their management offered little resistance to the outsourcing.

The clever politician looked the other way – after all, their golden parachute," if you will, was the taxpayer!

From a bird's perspective, one could easily recognize the four door black SUV as it thundered down the farm-to-market road near the famous Washington Crossing on the Delaware River.

The particularly severe winter of 1777-1778 proved to be a great trial for the American Army, and of the 11,000 soldiers stationed at Valley Forge, hundreds died from disease. However, the suffering troops were held together by loyalty to the Patriot cause and to General Washington, who stayed with his men.

Wow! What a Tribute to America and its history, Miguelito Pohlmann and the Band of Six would think thought Johannes, as he cushioned himself deeper into the self made foxhole at the junction of the country road that the three ton Cadillac SUV would travel.

The driver of the SUV thought only of finding and eliminating Johannes, and their Employer gave them "Carte Blanche" also to kill the Healer. The Driver's fixation caused him to graze a large very old oak tree dating back to those revolutionary war days.

The big Cadillac swerved to avoid hitting another one. The others yelled: "yuh Mother Fucker", the term of endearment used by many in the big city Ghettos, ya gonna keel usss awl!"

They were not sure of the location coordinates furnished to them by Alistair. Hearsay and unreliable home address information of the Human Resources Department was also provided to the Band of Six.

Clabbard or clapboard houses of colonial period vintage were common in the area; house numbers, if any, would not be visible from the road.

She had saved him from Satan's grip. She knew it.

He was totally exhausted, as he lay bleeding on the wooden floor.

He awakened suddenly, he looked at her.

She was a beautiful Entity! Her skin colour was of a mixture of black and brown, it shone brightly in her rather round face. Her physical side was strong yet shapely.

Johannes asked himself, am I still living?

His now wide open eyes saw pleasure, a desirable Creature in the truest sense of the word, as if she was transformed into a biblical wise person!

He recognized her! She came from Pakistan, actually she was a gynecologist, he had met her earlier in London on the occasion of a party given by her husband.

A wife of a former colleague, his name was Ahmed. At that time it was unknown that her actual birthplace was Cuba.

She also recognized him, smiling, glad that he was now awake and she could rescue him from his brief dance with the Devil.

She smiled broadly, and remembered that first time they had met, she knew he was no playboy, he exuded character and a personable nature of Faithfulness.

She touched him tenderly, when she rubbed an herbal salve deep into his wounds. She applied the bandages, he was clearly under her Spell, she behaved like a spiritual magician.

Her thick powerful fingers rubbed on his upper thighs more Salve to heal more quickly the already stitched up wounds.

Her softly applied hand movements danced over his naked body to allow him to be fully relaxed to ensure healing.

He then began to sense the familiar sensation in his lower extremities and the erection became quite pronounced. She smiled at her husband, and said: "Johannes, I am your Savior. I dedicate myself totally to your healing."

"Other activities between us come later. You know what I mean."

After her softly spoken words, he sighed deeply, relaxing his genitalia.

Ahmed came to him in Spirit, discussing how and why he suddenly died, saddening everyone who knew him.

Her first husband, Ahmed was a wonderful human being, a faithful man, one that always did for others, he was selfless. He was a 'Workaholic, spent insufficient time at home, and unfortunately died from Acquired Immune Deficiency Syndrome (AIDS), when an accident in the medical laboratory sprayed a small amount of infected blood on him. In those last days he suffered terribly.

He thought, fortunately for me, Ahmed was no Bum who would take advantage of her kindness and goodheartedness.

But Ahmed thought Alischraga should not work, remain as a housewife with children, and she should lose weight.

He was not jealous, but sincere in his beliefs about Hindu women.

Johannes and Alischraga were two half-Souls, now joined together in one Flesh; they lived in seventh heaven. It was good. It remained good.

He wanted her to still wear her traditional headscarf, she should be proud of her background and religion, Also wearing the headpiece revealed all the more so her beaming happiness exuding from her rather round mahogany colored face; she had accustomed herself to the absence of Ahmed.

Johannes, now forty nine years old, slept the entire night. He dreamed of her who took extreme pains to look after him, she explained many things to him talking to him as he slept, she continued to whisper in his ear, she hovered over him like a helicopter, her gleaming black eyes ranged up and down over his wounded body – hypnotically.

She wanted nothing to go wrong.

Astonishing, thought Johannes subconsciously. Alischraga Saleh. My sweet Alischraga!

He remembered when he first met "Ali."

After the Cremation, they moved into the new apartment, covered totally in Italian designed tile. They did not like carpet, it retained too much dust and allergens, even after a thorough cleaning.

The guests at their wedding had tears of joy for the couple, this time the wedding was not arranged by their parents – true feelings of love and respect were evident.

Alischraga declared: "I am carried away in respect and love for my Johannes."

Johannes said it was love at first sight, he saw her for the first time cross the street wearing a dark green Sari, she was above average height, her black eyes met his, they stared momentarily at each other, within a few seconds they knew each other!

They never forgot that moment.

Johannes admitted, that he had not been nervous. Alischraga fulfilled his strongest expectations of his dream woman.

She had no butterflies in her stomach, she instantly knew he was the complete man - perfect in every respect.

In contrast to others, they never argued, and they knew immediately that they wanted to spend the rest of their lives together.

Alistair and Fernanda wanted to tear apart this very happy couple, they knew too much about their dishonest behavior, and their escape unnerved them.

Miguelito observed the happy Couple.

The Sun would rise again for them, like the first time.

They would wake up each day as if they were born again. Renewed with vigor, smell the air and the flowers, and go to work as if they were about to attend the first day of school.

Miguelito harbored other thoughts.

He thought also of his victory in battle over those Shitbags. Now there would be fewer jerks in the world.

He looked at the piled up naked corpses. The scars on their skin seemed to emanate from long periods of torture – the women more than the men.

Their uniforms were similar to those of another time.

But the engraved initials, which appeared on the back sides of their black shirts, belonged to one of the largest agencies of the US Government!

He looked at the Full Moon, its Rays illuminated the surrounding bushes and brush, the uneven character of the thick bushes from a horizontal viewpoint resembled a sawtooth shadow.

He eyed the corpses, then stomped out the small trickle of blood with his calf length combat boots, first the right one, then the left.

The dried blood looked like dried dog feces, the low air humidity transformed it into dust which the wind would soon carry away into the atmosphere.

Miguelito thought that it is always bad to lose good people to the Devil.

The spiritual concept of Karma – every good and bad act has a consequence, becomes manifest in the next life.

Miguelito said to the happy couple: Si. El Karma es una Arpia", that is: Karma's a Bitch!"

Miguelito lit a match, and threw it on the pile of lifeless human meat.

The flames ripped through the bodies, the smell of smoked barbeque meat filled the air, but with one exception, there was no BBQ Sauce!

Before they met their maker, perhaps they enjoyed their last Meal of Platanos Maduros!

White hot coals of residue remained, after an hour, the ashes disappeared in the air.

He raised his eyebrows while he shook off the white dust from his boots, and said: a cheap cremation for these idiots, the situation warranted no shedding of tears."

The Day's events weighed heavily on his lungs. He reached for his backpack and pulled out a substantial amount of wild grass and weeds, picked by hand out of the sand dunes.

He threw the mixture into a large iron pot of boiling water, let it boil for fifteen minutes, and allowed another fifteen minutes for this home made Tea to cool.

An old Sailor's recipe, it cleans the lungs in a manner that retains the light pure salt air of the Caribbean Region.

Miguelito saw a deteriorating environment for law enforcement.

Satan and his minions were undermining the Law and Order of this wonderful country.

He and others of the Army of the Lord would have to take measures in their own hands to restore the God-given rights of Liberty and Justice for all peoples.

Quitting is not an option for a soldier in the Army of the Lord.

THE REMNANT FAITHFUL -SOLDIERS OF THE LORD

Miguelito Pohlmann, the Spoiler of the Assassination Plot against his friends, loved the Excitement of Battle against Evil.

After his shootout with the Band, he hummed the lyrics of the James Bond film – "Live and Let Die."

He noted that the lyrics resembled greatly his Quest for this Job, and how he sent his enemies to Hell, it was business as usual –live and let die instead of live and let live.

The world changed daily- he knew that the only constant in this life besides death and taxes, was change.

And, that was good. We are becoming less secular.

We were slowly going back to God, back to respecting and honoring him. More common sense, less political correctness, thought Miguelito.

He mused further about the lack of preparedness on the part of the Band. To win, thought Miguelito, one must not wait for the enemy to attack; instead, throw the enemy out before a foothold is gained.

The Holy Ghost had spoken to Miguelito, saying: "if Al Capone was kicked out of Chicago early on, when he was just a small time

244

operator, he would not have had the opportunity to create so much havoc."

"But the Devil slowed the people's anger against this petty jerk, until he became so powerful, and corrupted so many; it took an Army of the Remnant Faithful – law abiding and God fearing enforcers to bring him to heel."

Miguelito knew also that the Devil was out to destroy his friends and anyone who stood against him. He took the initiative and attacked – they hadn't expected it.

Those still living in Cuba under the Yoke of Communism regret not chasing out the fledgling Rebels before they became too entrenched in people's minds

But one question haunted him. Why was this heavily armed group so easily surprised and overcome?

They enjoyed the best of training and military combat experience. Also, Rosa enabled them!

Ah! That was the answer, perhaps.

Rosa showered them with many perks. The ready access to Marijuana in all forms was welcomed by the group – the three women viewed the reefers as "stimulating," and it made them horny as all get out.

What the Band did not know was the continued use of hashish accentuated their PTSD, impaired their memory and concentration!

After surviving the ordeal, Johannes discussed with Miguelito his escape and how the events unfolded during the evening. He could not recall everything, as Miguelito reminded him that he almost died that evening.

Miguelito also provided his friend with what he saw and did that evening.

Johannes was almost out of breath when he slipped on the damp grass running from the Band. His Meniskus had slipped sideways again in his left knee area.

The pain was sharp and the swelling was pronounced. He fell on his right knee in the soft ground, and rolled into the ditch adjoining the hedgerows.

He heard the raucous laughter behind him. Did they actually see him fall into the ditch? Were they laughing at him?

He was bleeding profusely from several AK 47 rounds fired at him. They saw him fall into the ditch, but it was now dusk and he would be hard to find.

He began to rub the spasm that impacted his left upper thigh around the knee area, the result of a strained hamstring muscle. To further relax the area, he engaged a hip loosening exercise that he learned in yoga class. After a while, he might be able to run again.

He heard them suddenly stop chasing him.

The motor of their orange colored hummer H3 Alpha stopped, their in total 800 pounds bodyweight caused the vehicle to still rock from side to side –vibrating, as they climbed out.

Despite the darkness of night, one could still see the gold crucifix that hung on the inside mirror, vibrate, the approximate two karat diamond etched in the middle of the crucifix gleamed prominently in the moonlight.

The brilliant shining solid gold crucifix appeared to have an antique hue and design. Was this a plundered item from the Iraqi National Museum in Baghdad?

Had the Band participated in the plundering of over 170,000 artifacts from the Museum's basement, a serious crime against humanity, if true?

It was midnight, and the smoking of several Joints began to take effect.

They casually rolled the dice and took bets that their easy prey would bleed to death, and they would find his rigor mortis set body the next day.

The group began to engage in foolish and idle talk, became lethargic and soon their interests narrowed to more pleasurable thoughts.

Curious, Johannes pulled himself slowly up to the edge of the ditch to see what the Band was doing.

He saw the female members of the group talk among themselves, and began to slither out of their clothes. More silly talk and giggling could be heard.

They moved in unison toward the now naked male members of the group, as all now displayed their erect manhood.

They were all as high as Kites!

They clashed, and the transparency of a "cluster fuck," an orgy of passion, came in full view.

In complete surprise Johannes saw Miguelito, also unexpected by the group, walk softly over to the pile of clothing, guns, laptops, smart phones, and he very quietly picked up the items.

Their orgy would not last forever, as he positioned himself to view the "three dirty legs and the three hardlegs" - all six from a position of a surprise attack.

Miguelito spoke to this Riff Raff with the language that only they would fully understand: "Quitate, Hijos de Puta! Vamos a entrar!"

The group, now aware of his presence, searched frantically for their firepower, as they saw him raise his Remington handheld 12 Guage shotgun toward them, he delivered six rounds from about 10 yards out, all striking their targets, the impact of the 00 buckshot threw them backwards several feet.

During the foray, one could hear Miguelito hum the lyrics of a certain Scandinavian heavy metal band as he rapidly re-loaded and let loose another barrage of buckshot to hold his opponents at bay.

There was now no movement among the rag doll like bodies lying on the hard cold ground.

The foolishness and uncleanliness of their actions brought to mind Chapter 5 of the book of Ephesians, reasoned Miguelito.

Johannes struggled to climb from his hiding place, and limped toward his friend. Earlier he had been wounded several times with rapid fire from AK -47s by the Band.

After about 200 yards of slow walk and pause and limping action toward his loyal friend, whom he had not expected to show up to rescue him and his Alischraga from the bestial oriented warriors hired by Alistair and Rosa, he collapsed about five feet from the pile of naked shot up bodies.

Miguelito looked down at his victims, and muttered that the

wild bunch picked a bad time to go after the happy couple as two planets named Rahu and Kehtu were in full swing.

Although the two planets are not visible to the naked eye, the influence which they can exert on people's lives is immense.

The planets'transit lasts for a period of around 18 months. People get good or bad results in accordance with their past karma, which is signified by planets like Rahu and Ketu.

During the planets' transit there can be a quick rise or sudden downfall in peoples' prospects.

He looked again at the bodies. He noticed that their eyes remained open, he did not close them.

Interesting, he thought. Some indicated a smile; perhaps they were in the midst of getting "off," when the 00 buckshot load struck.

He carefully removed all of their dog tags, driver's licenses, and other identity documents. Their black uniforms on the damp ground exhibited a patch on each arm showing a firey tail of a Boa Constrictor, indicating the private security firm that employed them.

He would now tend to his friends' needs first before disposing of the human trash.

Those sons of bitches shot him.

He reached for the door handle of their SUV, opened the door, picked up the 185 pound Johannes from the damp ground and placed him in the SUV, floored the gas pedal, tires spinning on the gravel road to the abandoned factory and warehouse where the healer hid herself.

He placed him on a soft palett covering the wooden plank floor where distribution activities had previously taken place. Of course, those jobs were long gone – sacrificed to the idolatry of cheap labor.

The idolatrous men and women of the Government, thought Miguelito, were the same ones that endeavored to control the internet, put through gun control, initiate open borders to create the New World Order.

"New crises to cause doubt and stir fear, is out of Satan's playbook. It is an absolute and reliable Political Strategy for us," assured Alistair his idolatrous audience of security analysts and institutional investors.

Alistair assured the very secular thinking group that the new IPO would harvest millions of Dollars, since the government contracts were already consummated, and the giant Irradiation operation of Secure Systems would also provide incentives for the large factory farms to irradiate all of their produce.

As a producer also of portable and transportable irradiators to be placed in all agricultural fields and hothouses, the possibilities of future cash flows were endless!

Import laws were strengthened in favor of the irradiation of all products entering the country.

"We want to protect the public from foods produced in countries where cleanliness standards are hardly observed."

"In short, protect and save American lives!"

Where have we heard this type of crap before, mused Miguelito.

The facts and the truth did not support the endless Charade

of the globalist CFF as Johannes and his team discovered through their very thorough examination of the MPAG, New York branch.

The Team discovered the seeds of evil doing via the "again and again" espoused propaganda of these powerful swindlers which demonstrated that the public can still be tricked into something unpleasant in the long run for them.

For example – better life, cheaper goods, in reality the reward for going along unknowingly with the concept of jobs exported overseas rendering better paying jobs almost obsolete, similar to that saying – the last Coke in the Desert!

The usual suspects reveled in the Land of Coca Cola, America, America, beautiful homes with large green lawns, neighbors struggling to keep pace with the Jonses, some even complaining about the neighbors grass patches covered with weeds!

This propagandized idolatry would be inclusive of legal and illegal drug addiction, the so called free market, Helicopter Ben and his ilk, toothless regulation, that is, little, if any enforcement against the law breakers, toxic mortgage assets, shoddy work environment on factory farms, greedy management seeking to cover up the transgressions of false labeling of irradiated and genetically modified foodstuffs, and add to these negatives: the deteriorating Center City social conditions, lack of restraint on false advertising of cash flow heavy medications and their deleterious side effects, can form a dangerous Cocktail of mutually exclusive outcomes.

The usual suspects, conditioned in childhood by overindulgent parents fall prey to the planned ways of Satan, thereby risking the loss of the inborn spirit of the Holy Ghost.

These thoughts haunted Johannes as he lay severely wounded on a section of wood floor in the abandoned factory.

To be sure, he was fighting for his life because of the suffering endured by the several large AK 47 bullet holes in his body fired by the veterans of that unjust Iraqi invasion.

Miguelito saw blood begin to come out of his mouth, coughing violently, before the healer could rush to his side.

His breathing became labored, before she could wipe the blood from his face. Suddenly, she heard no breathing from him.

My Johannes!

She screamed endlessly. Then she stopped as quickly as soon as her tears of anguish had begun.

She noticed that his blood which had seeped into the tiny hairs of her left forearm began to dry on her muscular forearms and hands.

She removed her head scarf and began to lick his wounds; his blood still had life, pure and free from any guilt. Then she wiped the area clean.

Miguelito opened the almost rusted through front door, his muscular shadow spanned the width of the opening, and he saw the motionless body of his friend, his Alischraga next to him.

He knew that she was so much in love with him.

Now these corrupt Shitheads "bumped him off!"

She still wiped and licked his bloody wounds, like a Cat, traces of his blood on the soft rim of her mouth could be seen.

They were one Flesh, she was with him, suffered with him and hoped to bring him back to life.

Without warning, he opened his eyes! Earlier his heart quit beating. But now!!

His eyes were clear and sparkled with Joy!

Then he whispered in her tastefully perfumed ear: "My precious Angel, I love you so much!"

He said: "I survived the attack! This is not my last adventure! They can't get rid of me so easily!"

Alischraga's Face beamed with Joy!

The couple embraced passionately, her tears of Joy streamed over and down her smooth mahogany colored cheeks, her scant makeup was no longer visible.

Johannes and Alischraga thanked the Holy Father and his Son for their Redemption.

Others of their supervision group were not so fortunate.

Two years before, they attended a funeral for their close friend, Ian Herzeleid.

His Jewish colleague requested his Rabbi to read a prepared statement to the group attending the funeral.

The Rabbi read: "My years with the Federal Reserve System were for the most part good years. However, the System began to hire many people who did not observe the best interests of the System."

"These evil people came mostly from domestic banks, and harassed not only me, but others, as they endeavored to destroy the original supervisory purpose of the founding of the FRB System, and eliminate the regulatory function."

"I now carry the Injustice of these evil people to my final resting place."

"When will a handshake between people once again signify honesty and commitment?"

It was rare to see someone among the attendees who did not experience sadness and tears.

Outside the funeral home, the rain pounded the ground and the air smelled like fresh flowers.

Without hesitation Miguelito thought of the Mark Twain quote: "Everyone is a full moon, and has a dark side which no one wants to show."

His guardian Angel brought him back to life, and said to him: "peace in this world is very short, since the condition of the heart of the world is not dedicated to Holy Love of one another."

"The corrupted heart leads to Chaos, which tolerates Evil. Against that, one must every day fight Satan's deceit and fraud."

"Do not fall for the confusion of Satan's minions – the demand for new types of packaged foods, medicatons to heal the body and innovative financial instruments requiring regulatory approval – which do not in practice, observe the time tested admonition: "Caveat Emptor."

Mass produced consumer goods do not assure quality and stability of profit.

Like an earthquake, they try to traumatize us, but we do not live unprotected! I have a few ideas how we can overcome this Satanic organization, but we must first hide ourselves in a friendly land."

After bathing herself, she stood watch over her Johannes when he submerged himself in the healing waters of the Ganges, to wash away his Sins and reflect on recent changes in his life during the traditional Kumbh Mela Pilgrim Festival – the largest religious gathering in the world.

Then they walked two miles back to their hotel, where he performed his trusted yoga movement to enhance his spiritual equilibrium.

He moved slowly and smoothly across the room, legs and arms contorting in a movement to promote the circuitry in his brain, bringing the spiritual and the physical in harmony, to relax and ease the healing of muscular tears and sprains and other painful experiences.

Back in New York City, Rosa and Alistair received special invitations for wine tasting and gourmet foods sampling.

This gastronomic Event was hosted by none other than the Super Chef, who still enjoyed a mixed Notoriety.

She smiled and waved at Alistair as she remembered the Good Old Days of insider trading, she provided many 'hot tips' to him and Rosa, as she performed her broker role with a major trading house.

With great skill, she indulged all of her guests with the finest culinary delicacies.

She belonged to that group of usual suspects who were able to create manufactured crises, volatility and enormous trading profits.

Ahhh, she sighed, it was good to be part of this up and coming GROUP!

This generation found little value in the retention of historical information, cultural treasures and their epochal ideas.

In reality, they wanted to destroy such history which did not coincide with their strategic Globalism and re-write history to their own liking.

Even going so far as to utter such nonsense that their country's constitution and declaration of independence based on Christian Principles did not provide the foundation for greatness.

A secular thinking world was their foundation for global greatness, which they, of course, would determine.

There was no room for religious thinking, only their ungodly ideas would become the basis for their version of global greatness – a New World Order!

They must be stopped!

However, Johannes longed for other days; when biblical teachings were revered and respected – a blueprint for the orderly conduct of Society – the basis for taking a stand against disorderly circumstances fostered by Satan.

He hated that generation of the usual suspects that endeavored to cause crises of confidence in major financial and economic sectors; their secular ideas paid little attention to an orderly society, backed by satanical behavior they would create a watered down regulatory environment. They would quash any resistance to their ideas of how the world should be.

Johannes knew that the team's disclosure of the unsatisfactory operational condition of the MPAG New York branch, the linchpin of the Frankfurt, Germany private bank for global activities, could bring about its demise as a major player in the global financial system.

Simone disclosed all of the mythical objections to thorough examination procedures, follow through, and punishment of the perpetrators of fraudulent activities in those three most important economic sectors.

She outlined the full disclosure of Alistair's insider trading activities and Fernanda's disgraceful supervisory behavior.

Simone's findings were not a figment of her imagination.

Her review of the compliance department also reflected questions about the long term viability of its function, and if it could survive another round of intense scrutiny.

The mess in the Compliance Department had its origin at least three years ago. Certain examiners sat on their backsides with their eyes closed since the remedial work required meant writing up more frigging reports, and presenting to the Board their case why this branch should lose its banking license.

Nothing happened.

This time, the heavy criticism could no longer be ignored!

Simone, like Johannes, became a target to be assasinated; her findings could, if made available to the other regulators, result in serious monetary penalties – a punishment long favored by government securities regulators, in their own strategy, that was more preferable to supervisory action requiring consistent employment of examiner resources to review corrective actions.

The fraudulent reporting of sufficient capital funds to offset losses could result in a fine of US$ One million per day until the amount reached the required Capital of US$50 milliion for US operations.

In this connection, the branch management would have to increase its capital as the cheapest way to avoid undue credit losses, instead of relying on more review of operations weaknesses and their immediate resolution.

Even more damaging to the team was the disclosure to the Board of Directors of the Third District, that two of their own had violated Ethical Rules of Conduct – more than the mere appearance of wrong doing!

The report, if read by the Board would provide painful reading!

He looked at Alischraga and stated:"Nothing New," but his words were premature, as he suddenly heard the roar of a massive Food Truck that paused and stopped in front of them.

He saw the driver. A muscular broad shouldered type that he had seen before. He wore a striped shirt and a paisley tie.

The driver grinned at them.

Then the huge truck painted in dark red with flaming black stripes on each side drove off in a southerly direction to access one of several interstate highway systems.

It was BILL!

Earlier they discovered Simone's undercover activity. It was in plain view in one of the more dynamic cities in the fast growing southeastern part of the United States.

Strolling through the large Plaza of the Wells Fargo Regional Headquarters, they observed the long line of customers waiting for their fast food fare. However, it was no ordinary fast food, prepared fresh in front of the long line of office building employees.

The name on the Food Truck was appropriate: The Dumpling Food Truck – and the large portions in the form of wraps, cups of soup, salads, etc. were prepared by two rather comely looking women - one in particular exhibited long black braids, she saw us and winked with her extra long eyelashes!

Simone! They pretended not to recognize her.

"Now we have to locate Rich and Susan?"

And, who of the former team of five might betray them?

Few of the public dared to arrest the ususal suspects of the CFF; they still remained in positions of power, controlled the media and vowed to continue their dangerous and reckless strategy.

CPSIA information can be obtained
at www.ICGtesting.com
Printed in the USA
LVHW031243240619
622139LV00003B/567